SWALLOW YOUR *fear*

KARLEY BRENNA

*For the girls who want their cowboys a little dark.
I hope Booker and his friends fulfill some of those fantasies
for you.*

And for Rose. I think I like the dark side.

IMPORTANT NOTE

Dear Reader,

While Swallow Your Fear is clearly labeled as a dark romance, I never want anyone going into a book without the option of reading the triggers. Please know that some of these may contain spoilers to specific scenes:

Torture, graphic violence, light stalking, breaking & entering/trespassing, waterboarding, masked men, murder, on-page gun use, mention of gambling, domestic violence, cheating (not by either of the MCs), kidnapping, and a haunted house scene. On-page kinks include degradation, breath play, exhibitionism, primal play, masochism, nipple play, group scenes, and rope play.

CHAPTER 1

BOOKER

"Maybe we can use this as the murder weapon," Henley said after handing me the pliers.

I shook my head, maneuvering the pliers around where I'd tied the barbed wire together. "You think killing the guy will get you out of this?" Out of all of us, Henley had the least amount of brain cells, and it showed. Between his gambling addiction and his special ability to constantly get himself in a bind that only Austin or I could get him out of, I was damn close to kicking him off this damn ranch for good. But Austin, Henley, and I were friends, brothers by choice, so I had to stick by him regardless of whether I agreed with his decisions or not. It'd been that way between the three of us since elementary school, and we'd been glued together since.

In the silver shadow cast by the moon high in the sky, he shrugged. "If he's dead, we'd get the deed back."

Using the pliers, I tightened the knot. After finishing up fixing the break in the fence, I stood, holding the tool out to his chest. "Not betting the fucking deed to my ranch

1

in the first place would've kept it in our goddamn hands to begin with."

Austin chuckled from where he was perched on his horse behind us. "Oh, come on, Booker. We all knew Henley was due for a little shit stirring."

"It's *our* ranch," Henley corrected, taking the pliers from me. He wasn't wrong—all three of us technically owned the five-hundred-acre property together, but that didn't give him free rein to bet our home in a childish game of pool.

"And it's *your* problem. Fix it." Brushing by him with a swipe of my shoulder, I grabbed the horn of the saddle, stuck a boot in the stirrup, and mounted my horse, Onyx. He was nearly nineteen hundred pounds of pure muscle, always up for whatever demanding task we had on the ranch, so when I'd tacked him up at one a.m. after a neighbor stopped by to tell us our cows were on the road, he hadn't protested one bit.

"He cheated," Henley stated, getting on his own horse.

I grunted in response as Austin snorted.

"He did," Henley defended, trotting up next to us.

"Got proof?" I asked, mentally kicking myself for entertaining this. It wasn't the first time Henley had tried to get us to help him get out of a bind. This time, it just involved the roof over our fucking heads. *No biggie.*

"Well, no, but—"

"Here we go again," Austin muttered.

"But," Henley continued, sending a glare Austin's way. "He's cheated before, I know it. So if we just scare him a bit, maybe it'll make him give it back."

I felt bad for him. I did. And I'd have his back through

this, like we always did. But why not bet a fucking cow or something? "Why the fuck did you even bring the deed with you to begin with?"

Henley shrugged, head downcast on his horse's mane. "Had nothing else to bet."

"So ask me for a twenty or something," Austin said, his tone a bit softer now.

"Don't bet in the first place," I grumbled.

Henley shook his head. "It's more high stakes than that."

"Maybe stop getting yourself involved in that shit, then?" I offered, like that wasn't an obvious fucking option. It wasn't his fault, though, really. He got the habit from his dad and couldn't kick it. The piece of shit brought him along to some of the most dangerous situations, so Henley got a taste for it young. He loathed his father for it, but liked the thrill. The *what if I win* pounding in his brain with every gamble.

He ignored my comment, like I knew he would. "He's got this girlfriend—she works at Marv's Diner."

Even under Austin's cowboy hat, I saw his brows raise in Henley's direction. "What do you suggest we do with this girlfriend of his, Henley? Rough her up? We don't mess with girls. Not like that."

"No!" Henley said hurriedly. "No. We're not going to hurt her. But maybe he visits the diner she works at. We could corner him there, scare him a bit."

"You're suggesting we use her as bait?" It wasn't the worst idea, so long as we didn't involve the girl. Either way, we had to get the deed back. I wasn't giving up this ranch over a fucking game of pool.

"Not bait. More like a lure," Henley said.

Austin chuckled again. "Same fucking thing, dipshit."

We didn't typically give Henley this much shit, but between him coming home at five in the afternoon plastered beyond comprehension, his dropped bomb of betting the deed away, and being woken up in the middle of the night for cows on the road, we were both a bit irritated—to put it lightly.

Henley let out a sigh. "Fine. Whatever you want to call it. We stake out the diner, wait until he shows up, and take care of it then."

"And if he doesn't show up?" Austin asked.

I waited for Henley to respond, and when he didn't, I glanced his way.

"We find him instead," he finally answered.

There was no telling what I'd do to protect Austin, Henley, and this ranch. I'd find this asshole, put him in his place, and make sure Henley stayed far the fuck away from any more gambling opportunities. Once the deed was in my hands, I'd make sure none of the guys could find it, lest Henley get any more brilliant ideas.

Leaning down to open the gate, I said, "I'll head over there tomorrow."

"I can come with," Henley offered.

I swung it wide as Onyx side-stepped to let Austin and him pass. "Not a chance."

Henley angled his horse toward me as I shut the gate. "Why not?"

Once the latch was back in place, I straightened, heading in the direction of the barn. "You think he's not going to be suspicious if he sees you there?"

"I doubt he remembers me," Henley said.

We stopped in front of the lit up barn, the light illuminating the surrounding area. Everything else was nearly nonexistent with the faint hue from the moon. Austin dismounted, getting to work on his latigo. "Hen, if I had to guess, you were the plastered one, not him. He knew exactly what he was doing, taking advantage of you."

Henley and I followed suit. I just wanted to go the fuck back to bed, not be standing out here talking about Henley's bad decisions. That was a conversation for *after* coffee, not before.

I glanced over Onyx's back at Henley. The mopey look on his face wasn't sitting right with me. "What happened?"

He looked up. "What do you mean?"

"Why'd you do it?" Henley had made some stupid decisions in the past, but this beat all of them by a long shot.

He shrugged, taking his sweet time on the latigo. "Aubree and I ended things, and I just... I drank too much and wasn't thinking. Thought if I lost her, I had nothing else to lose."

Austin and I paused, leaving the cinches dangling from our saddles.

"Why didn't you tell us?" Austin asked. We always went to each other with anything, regardless of what it was.

Henley took his hat off, setting it on the horn of his saddle. "I don't know. I wasn't thinking. Stopped by here to clear my head and thought 'fuck it' and ended up at the pool hall with the deed. Lost it to some asshole cheat named Chase."

All three of us stood there a moment, letting it sink in, the only sound the crickets chirping in the fields. It was chilly being the middle of fall here in Whiskey Ridge, but no extreme temperature drops yet. One look at the grand farmhouse sitting a mere thirty yards from the barn sent a shiver down my spine, despite the layers I had on. We couldn't lose the property. It was our livelihood, and without it, we'd be lost. Three men with no place to call home.

"We'll get it back," I told him, hefting the saddle off.

"You guys really don't need to get involved. I can do it myself," Henley said, shame coating his words.

Austin shook his head, setting a hand on Henley's shoulder. "We're in it together, Hen. We'll figure it out."

With a nod, we finished up, untacking the horses and putting them away before heading inside to get some rest. We all sure as fuck needed it with the unknown of what was to come tomorrow.

CHAPTER 2

BOOKER

"I'd much rather have the booth," Austin mumbled as we followed the waitress through the run-down diner.

The blonde gestured to the small table in the center of the restaurant, her high ponytail swinging over her shoulder as she faced us. "Here you are."

"Thank you, ma'am," I said, ignoring Austin's complaint and taking the seat facing the kitchens. The table gave us a clear view of the entire diner, including the front doors.

He sat across from me as she asked, "Can I get you two started with anything?"

"Waters, please." We wouldn't be eating, but the last thing I needed was her complaining we didn't order anything to her coworkers and bringing us unnecessary attention.

She set the menus in front of us. "I'll be right back with those."

Austin noticeably watched her ass sway in her tiny skirt, his head turned her way until she disappeared into the kitchen. Once she was gone, he faced me. "What's the plan?"

"Not fucking the entire waitstaff," I said, surveying the diner. It wasn't in the best shape, but not much in Whiskey Ridge was. Most of the cushioned seats were torn, scratches etched into the wobbly tables, and the windows looked like they hadn't been cleaned in years. I didn't want to guess what the state of the kitchen was, and it made me all the more thankful we'd eaten before we came.

"I wasn't going to bang her," Austin defended.

I arched a suspecting brow.

"Alright. I thought about it," he admitted.

I shook my head. He was like a kid in a candy store in these places, and the short skirts were teasing him like samples of taffy. "We're going to wait until this guy's girlfriend shows her face, then wait to see if he comes by for a visit."

Henley had brought us up to speed before we'd left this morning. He'd shown us pictures of the girlfriend off Chase's social media, as well as what he looked like so we'd know who to keep an eye out for. He'd mentioned he had a knife on his belt during the match, which meant he knew trouble could present itself at any turn. We just had to hope he wasn't prepared for it today.

"I know that," he said, leaning back in his chair. The metal creaked under the shift in his weight. "But after. Say he does show up. Then what?"

I shrugged. I hadn't thought that far ahead, but whatever ended up happening, if he wouldn't hand the deed back, I had no doubt it'd turn ugly. I wasn't afraid to get my hands dirty if it meant keeping us above water. We had to stick out for our own out here, and I had no ties to Chase to give a damn what happened to him in the fallout.

I folded my hands in my lap, leaning back against the uncomfortable metal posts of the chair, and kept an eye on both the door and the kitchen. "We'll do what Henley suggested."

As Austin shook his head despite the devilish glint in his gaze, the blonde waitress came back with our waters. "Ready to order?"

"We need a minute," I answered, not glancing her way.

Austin, on the other hand, was practically drooling as he looked up at her. "Thanks, McKenna."

After she walked away, I shook my head and said, "Typical name move."

"Her name tag is right out in the open." Austin surveyed out the windows behind me, watching the street. "Not my fault women are suckers for when a guy says their name."

"I'm not sure they mean like that," I stated.

"Oh, yeah? Then what do they mean?"

"When they're not around you, for starters," I said as the door to the kitchen swung outwards, blocking the worker from my view.

"Bullshit." Austin folded his arms, defensive. He was too easy to rile up. He was also too good at getting girls' attention with his sharp jaw, signature five o'clock shadow, and just-long-enough-to-look-messy hair.

The door swung shut, revealing a familiar brunette with blonde tips. "Brynne."

"Don't go testing the name out on your tongue, now," Austin grumbled.

"No, dumbass." I nodded in the direction of the mostly empty bar as Brynne took the order of an old, wiry-haired man. "Chase's girlfriend is right there."

Austin twisted in his seat, and I slapped a palm to my face. *Way to be fucking discreet.*

"Oh, shit." He faced me again. "Guess timing worked out in our favor."

The front door flung open, its foggy glass making it hard to see who walked through. As they stormed in, I wasn't sure who I was expecting, but it wasn't Chase. It was almost too easy. Our target just entered like a bat out of hell, and I was almost glad for the mood he seemed to be in. It'd make this a hell of a lot more fun.

Brynne stood there, finishing writing down the order despite Chase's blazing glare. He practically shoved the old man off his seat as he braced his hands on the edge of the bar. "Outside. Now."

She didn't look up from the notepad. "Little busy."

His arms, not quite impressive in their size, bulged slightly as he gripped the counter. *"Now."*

She raised her chin, regarding him with a bored gaze. "Is there something I can get you?"

"Brynne's taking her break," Chase shouted toward the back before turning and leaving the diner.

I watched, waiting to see her next move, as Austin mumbled, "That doesn't sound good."

If she followed, I'd have to do the same. I couldn't risk Chase leaving before I confronted him.

Brynne ripped the paper off her pad, setting it on the shelf for the cook to find, and refilled the elderly man's water glass. *She wasn't going to leave.*

But then, she untied her waist apron, set it on the counter, walked around the end, and disappeared out the front door.

"Goddamnit," I muttered, the chair scraping along the linoleum floor as I stood.

Austin went to stand as well, but stopped when I held a hand out.

"Stay here. I'll be right back."

I didn't stick around to see if he listened as I beelined it out of the diner, checking both ways down the cracked sidewalk to see where they'd gone. But I didn't have to look for long before a woman said, "Let me go, Chase."

"All your shit is gone," Chase spit back from down in the alley beside the diner. I stayed out of view, listening from the corner.

"Why do you think that is?" Brynne snapped back.

"If you found another man—"

"If *I* did? You're the one who's slept with half the damn town since getting with me. I had to find out through McKenna!"

"Maybe if you'd do your job in bed, I wouldn't have to," he spit out.

That wouldn't slide.

Before I could think better of it, I stepped around the corner, and the scene before me nearly made me rip his hand clean off. He had her wrist pinned to the wall, his grip hard as her hand turned the slightest shade of purple.

I prowled toward them, and Chase's head snapped my way. "Little busy here, man."

Brynne's gaze found her shoes.

"Busy ignoring her request?" I asked, my words like knives wanting to find their target. Unfortunately for Chase, he was the blazing red bullseye.

"She's my girlfriend," Chase defended, and I swore, I was going to break his damn hand.

"I'm not your girlfriend," she murmured, refusing to look up.

Chase's eyes snapped to her, his face reddening. "What was that?"

His hand tightened on her wrist, and I snapped. Grabbing his arm, I tore it away from her, my other hand coming up to grip his wrist. I squeezed. Hard, just to see how he fucking liked it. "I think you heard her."

His eyes were frantic now as I backed him away from Brynne. I shouldn't give a damn. I was here to clean up Henley's mess, not whatever petty problems these two were having in their relationship.

"Let me go, man," Chase begged, and satisfaction rolled through me as his voice wobbled.

His back hit the brick wall on the opposite side of the alley, and I tightened my grip on his wrist further. "Did you let her go when she asked?"

His frenzied gaze landed on Brynne behind me. "Call for help!"

I nearly laughed. What a fucking wuss.

A crack echoed through the alley, and Chase yelled

out in pain as his wrist snapped under my hand. "You touch another woman without consent, and it won't just be your wrist I'm breaking." I let him go, his body shrinking into a ball as he crouched, cradling his broken bone.

I turned to find Brynne standing there, not a single emotion showing in her eyes. As soon as my back was to him, Chase stood up and darted, exiting the alley in a rush.

I lost my one shot, and now, Henley and I were both on his radar. My fists clenched at my sides before I headed back for the street.

"Thank you," Brynne said, pausing me in my departure.

Did she just thank me for breaking her ex-boyfriend's wrist?

"Not a problem," I replied, turning to look at her. She hadn't moved, her ponytail still draped over her shoulder. "That your ex?" Henley had told us they were still together, but based off what little of their conversation I'd overheard, they seemed to have broken up.

"As of last night, yes." She finally tilted her chin up, looking at me. My eyes dropped to her tiny skirt, far too much of her long legs on display. "He's mad I moved out and didn't tell him."

"I'd suspect any man would be." I didn't need to know their story. I just needed my fucking deed back.

Sticking out of the discreet pocket of her skirt was a chain, and I recognized the logo immediately. It was the only motel in town, and the state of the building was worse than the diner.

Without another word, I left, leaving her standing in

the alley. I wasn't going to try to comfort her. Last thing I needed was to get caught up in this bullshit any further.

I shoved open the door to the diner, finding Austin still sitting at the table. He had an elbow propped on the sticky surface, gazing up at McKenna as she popped her bubblegum.

"Time to go," I said, slapping a twenty on the table.

Austin did a double take before standing. "It was lovely speaking with you."

"You, too," McKenna said, shoving her hands in the front of her apron. "See you around."

We left the diner, and I didn't bother checking down the alley to see if Brynne was still standing there.

"I'm going to be busy tonight, so you and Henley need to take care of feeding," I said, rounding the front of my truck where it was parked on the street. We hopped in, and I started the engine.

"Where are you going?" he asked, buckling himself.

Pulling onto the street, I said, "Busy."

He snorted. "Always so open with me. What happened out there?"

"I broke the guy's wrist."

Out of the side of my eye, I saw Austin's brows skyrocket up his forehead. "You *what*?"

"He was about to do the same shit to her."

As if that was an excuse.

"Fucking hell, Booker. So not only do we need to clean up Henley's mess, but now yours, too?"

My hand twisted on the steering wheel. "I didn't create a mess."

"You broke his wrist. That sounds like a mess that needs cleaning."

"He probably pissed himself as he ran away, Austin. He's not going to cause a problem out of it."

He propped an elbow on the door. "You better fucking hope not. Now what are we supposed to do? You fucked up our only chance."

"I have a plan."

He threw his hands up in the air, then slapped them palms down on his jeans. "Lovely. Because that went so well the first time."

CHAPTER 3

BRYNNE

As if half of my belongings crammed in my car wasn't bad enough, a flat tire was just the cherry on top. I had no doubt Chase was the reason for this. He was a sore loser and that was one of the main reasons I left. Apparently, each time he'd lost a bet, he slept with a new girl in the vicinity. McKenna's sister had seen him fucking some chick in an alley, and I'd left not an hour after she'd told me. I could have gone to live with her, but she was in a one-bedroom house, and a couch didn't seem like my idea of comfort. Although, the motel mattress wasn't much of an upgrade.

And of course, Chase had hunted me down at work. I hadn't expected anything less. But slashing my tire? Major dick move.

After fishing through one of the bags in my car, I pulled out an oversized t-shirt and sweats. Before heading in the direction of the motel, I made sure to lock the doors, though nothing of value was in the vehicle. I'd taken a few things into the room last night, but left a good chunk of it on the backseat due to my desire to lose myself in a bottle of vodka.

By the time I got off work, it was dark, and the street-lamps were a joke as they cast a faint yellow glow over the weeds growing through the cracks in the sidewalk. This town could use some improvements, as well as the men in it. Whoever the man was that had intervened in the alley had broken Chase's wrist, but I wasn't sure if that really meant he was some kind of hero. By the sound of it, he had to have shattered the bone. The injury itself would make it difficult for Chase to play pool, which meant he'd have to win his earnings some other way. Otherwise, his boss would be pissed.

I didn't know exactly what Chase did to make money other than gambling, but half of what he won in the games he bet on went to the man he owed a debt to. That was all I knew, and even then, I wasn't sure why he had a debt with the guy. I wasn't even sure how much he owed, but by the time he'd already become invested in trying to pay the guy back, I could only guess that it had to be a lot.

The walk to the motel wasn't long at all, which was one positive out of this whole situation. If my streak of bad luck continued, I'd never make it through the week. Shifting the clothing to the crook of my arm, I fished the key out of the pocket of my skirt and inserted it into the knob. The hinge squealed as I shoved open the door, the room pitch black as I slipped inside. I closed the door behind me, making sure to lock it before I did anything else in case Chase followed me here. He wasn't normally so handsy, but his ego was hurt with me leaving, and by the act in the alley earlier, clearly he wasn't afraid to put a hand on me.

Feeling along the wall, I blindly searched for the light switch, running my hand up and down the textured wallpaper. Finally finding it, I flicked the switch, but as soon as the lights were on, a hand wrapped around my mouth, pulling me back into a stone hard chest. Instantly, I tried to grab for the attacker's arms, hands, anything, but they'd looped their other arm around my torso, holding mine flat to my sides.

Warm breath heated my neck as the intruder rested a stubbled chin on my shoulder, like my struggle was nothing. "Gotta calm down, Darlin'."

For the second time today, a man had his hands on me. My stomach twisted.

"Let me go," I tried to grit out beneath his hand, but my words were muffled. I tried to rear my leg up between his legs, but he was tall, and I hit nothing, only resulting in my skirt rising up my thighs even higher. I could kill Marv for making this our uniform.

"I just want to talk." His voice held no comfort as he dropped his hand from my mouth, and I swore it was familiar.

I grunted. "This isn't how you start a conversation."

"Would you suggest storming into your work instead?"

I knew exactly who the fuck this was.

The knowledge made me stop squirming. If he'd wanted to hurt me, he would have earlier. Right?

"Very good," he praised, his voice lower, smooth like barrel-aged whiskey.

Slowly, he released me, spinning me around so my back was to the wall. Unlike when I saw him in the alley, he now wore a skeleton mask that took up half his face, with a black cowboy hat casting him in a slight shadow.

"Are you scared, Brynne?" he asked, stepping closer as he tilted his head ever so slightly.

My breath hitched at the use of my name. I'd taken my name tag off, but I assumed he'd snuck a peek in the alley earlier.

I nodded. If that's how he wanted me to be, I wouldn't hide the fact that fear slithered over my skin like the mist that coated the air outside. How had he gotten in here?

"Good." He set a hand on the wall beside my head, leaning down. "I want you to listen very closely." His eyes, so dark behind the mask, devoured me where I stood. "Are you listening, Darlin'?"

I nodded again, at a loss for words.

"You're going to come live with me so I can take back what's mine."

He must be dreaming if he thought I'd go with him willingly. "Who even are you?" I spit.

"Your worst nightmare."

I wanted to roll my eyes despite the chill crawling over every inch of me. He wasn't doing a very good job compelling me to agree. If anything, the motel was a better motivator to take any opportunity I could get. "If that's the case, why would I agree to live with you?"

"Because if you don't, who knows what that wimpy little ex of yours will do next if I'm not there to save you."

Despite the close proximity, I crossed my arms over my chest and turned my nose up at him. "He's not going to come back."

The man let out a raspy chuckle, low and lacking humor. "You must not know him very well, then."

"I fucked the guy. I'd say I know him a hell of a lot better than you."

His hand darted up, grabbing my chin between his fingers. "You let some questionable men inside that pussy of yours. Not a good look."

My eyes narrowed as he kept my face firmly in place. He acted like he knew what men I'd slept with in the past. "I'm sure they're all a hell of a lot better than you. Bigger, too." The last remark was childish, but he was pissing me off.

He didn't let it get to him as he said, "He's a cheat." I tried not to let any emotion show on my face at the words as they stabbed me in the gut. "He plays dirty, but we play dirtier, Darlin'."

Who the fuck was *we*? Whatever his, or their, problem was, it wasn't mine. "How did you get into my room?"

He dropped my chin but didn't give me any space. "Real easy to pretend to be your boyfriend and get a key. Does that make you feel safe?"

It didn't. Not at all. He'd been able to get the key so effortlessly, and it only instilled how vulnerable I was here. Chase was mad, probably irate, about his broken wrist, and I had no doubt he'd figure out where I was staying and find a way in just as easily.

I could go to McKenna's, but Chase knew where she lived. Her house would be first on his list.

He stepped back, but no amount of distance could make the mask he wore any less frightening. That was the point, I supposed.

"You have twenty-four hours," he said, tossing the key on the comforter. "Otherwise, Chase won't be your only problem."

The door creaked on his way out, shutting with an ear-piercing scraping sound from the foundation having moved. The place was falling apart, and I seemed to be quickly following suit.

The fact that I was seriously considering taking a stranger up on his offer to live at his house baffled me. Not even a day ago, I would never have imagined myself in this situation, but now, I didn't seem to have a choice. I could stay in this piece-of-shit motel where anyone could pretend they knew me and get a key to my room, or I could live with a complete stranger. I had no other options. No family in town, no close friends other than McKenna. I was backed into a corner and desperate, which was exactly how this man wanted me to be.

Truthfully, I didn't have enough to stay in the motel longer than a week. Tips were shit at the diner, despite the revealing clothes my pig of a boss required for the dress code, and though the motel was trash, it wasn't cheap. But I had to persevere.

I landed face-first on the mattress, not bothering to change into the clothes I'd brought, and when sleep claimed me, I only saw that mask in my nightmares.

And it didn't end pretty.

CHAPTER 4

BRYNNE

"How'd your date go?" I asked McKenna as she refilled the napkin container at table four.

"Like absolute shit. Guy was a total sleaze-bag. You know, you really gotta go buy a new phone charger. I can't keep waiting to tell you things," McKenna replied.

"My phone has been dead for less than twelve hours," I pointed out. I'd forgotten my charger at Chase's house, and there was no way in hell I was going back for it.

She plopped the top back on the dispenser. "Twelve hours too long."

"I'll buy a new one after work." With what little tip money I made today. I was paying the motel by the day, so after today's expenses, I'd barely have enough for four more days. Magically overnight, my tire had replaced itself with a spare, and I had the slightest feeling I knew who'd fixed it. Whether I was right or not, I still wasn't going to take him up on his offer. I'd find a way to get by until I could rent somewhere, without that asshole's offer.

"Why don't you just go now?" McKenna asked, walking around the end of the bar to sidle up next to me.

I gave her a confused look. "Because I'm working?"

She shrugged, her mouth working on a piece of gum. "I won't tell on ya."

It was only thirty minutes before my shift was supposed to end, but... "I need the money."

"I'll clock you out in half an hour," she offered.

My eyes turned to slits as my skepticism set in. "Why?"

Her jaw moved as she likely debated telling me what she was thinking. I knew that look too well, being her best friend and all. "Because you look dead as a ghost and I know it's been a rough couple of days for you."

Rough was an understatement.

But half an hour more of sleep tonight would do me well. That was, if I even could sleep. The thought that anyone could get into my room at any moment didn't make a girl dream very easily.

"Okay, fine." I reached behind my back to untie my waist apron. "I owe you one."

She waved me off. "Don't worry about it. What are best friends for?"

Pulling the light blue apron off, I rolled it up into a ball and walked through the swinging doors to shove it in my locker. Marv didn't have any security cameras in the diner, so he wouldn't know I was leaving. The cook didn't know anything about our schedules, so for all he knew when he barely glanced up at me, I was supposed to be off anyway.

I offered him a closed-lip smile and headed out the back door. It slammed shut behind me, leaving me in the dark alley behind the restaurant with nothing but the blinking orange light to illuminate the wet pavement. It'd rained earlier, but now a chilly fog clung to the air, instantly cooling my exposed legs.

Every time the dying bulb flickered out, the narrow alley was cast in complete darkness. I kept my sights on the end as I walked in the direction of the street, where my car was still parked since the other night. Now that the tire was fixed, I'd drive it to the corner store, and grab a charger for my phone and a bottle of vodka to help me sleep. Once I was back at the motel, I'd figure out a way to barricade the door just in case someone did decide to break in—again.

I moved my gaze down to my white sneakers just as I narrowly missed a puddle, but when I looked forward again, I froze.

Standing at the end of the alley, blocking my only exit, stood a man in a cowboy hat, wearing the same skeleton mask as the night before.

Instantly, my body hummed as fear took over. He was just trying to scare me. He wouldn't actually—

He began moving, stalking toward me like a wolf stalked its prey, and I was the little helpless sheep with nowhere to go but straight into the hound's mouth. I took a step back, my sock instantly soaking through as my foot landed in the puddle. But I didn't care about that right now —not when I was about to be this man's victim.

"My coworker knows I'm out here," I called out, taking another step back.

He closed in on me, causing me to scramble backwards. A hand shot out, wrapping around my neck. I didn't have time to fight as he shoved me up against the wall and covered my mouth with a gloved hand.

Gloves. He was wearing *gloves*? He didn't want his fingerprints on me, which meant he was here to—

"Twenty-four hours is up, Darlin'." His voice was like spoiled honey, bitter and sweet at the same time, blissfully grating against my ears.

I tried to keep my breathing calm as he wrapped his hand tighter around my neck, still allowing me to breathe. Little clouds of white puffed out from my nose, evaporating between us.

"You only have one good choice here," he said. In the flickering light, his eyes were as dark as the alley behind him. "You want to tell me what your decision is?"

I nodded behind his hand, and he slowly eased up on the pressure. I swallowed, sucking in air. "I'm not going with you," I bit out.

His head cocked to the side slightly as he studied me. "That your final answer?"

I had a feeling that if I said yes, I'd end up a missing person or dead on the street. But something about him almost comforted me, like maybe he wouldn't *actually* kill me. I was playing with my life, and yet, I wanted to see how this ended.

"Yes."

His eyes held mine before they trailed down my cheek to my neck, where his hand was still carefully wrapped around the column. Slowly, he removed it, trailing a finger down my uniform. I kept my gaze on him, silently daring him to touch me inappropriately. As if he hadn't just had his hand around my fucking neck.

The tip of his finger swept over to my name tag still pinned to my button-up. "You can find out a lot about a person with just their name." His hungry eyes roamed further down, catching on my skirt. "Like where they live, where they work."

His attention moved back to my face, lingering on my parted lips. "What school they went to or who their friends are." He leaned closer, and the increase in my puffy breaths was all the indication he needed that he was succeeding in his plan of scaring me into submission. "I will always find you, Darlin'."

A finger came up to coast along the edge of my jaw, trailing up my chin to my bottom lip. He tugged down on it. "You think you're safe, that your perfect little world will go back to the way it was before you found out your little boyfriend was sleeping with half of Whiskey Ridge."

His finger let my lip pop back up, and he glided it down my chin again to trace the column of my throat. "And you're too scared to realize you have no choice but to accept my offer."

"I'm not scared," I said, finally speaking up.

The pad of his finger stopped right on my pulse point. "Your racing heart says otherwise."

I silently cursed my body for betraying me.

"I'll be generous and give you another day to decide." He dropped his hand, turning to walk away. The man stopped a few feet from me, looking over his shoulder. "But if I have to come find you again, I won't play nice."

He stared at me for a moment longer, letting his words set in, before the flickering light showed him leaving the alley. I stayed with my back against the wall until rain started falling, soaking me where I stood.

A crack of thunder had me hurrying to my car out

front. Once I was inside, I locked the doors and tried to scan my surroundings through the pelting rain.

But even without clear visibility, I knew he was out there watching.

And there was only one way to get him to leave me alone.

CHAPTER 5

BOOKER

Onyx walked ahead of Henley and Austin where they rode behind me. We'd gone out to double check the fence this evening, doing a better patch job than the other night. While we were out there, Henley and Austin had checked on the cows. I was right there with them, but all I kept seeing was that frightened look on Brynne's face, and how she'd looked so different than the fear that enveloped her in the alley that first day I saw her. She hadn't truly been scared of me. Not as the lower half of her body inched toward mine, her breasts perked up and distracting. She'd done it on purpose, but it was the things her body did that she didn't see that only drew me in more. That button nose turned up with flared nostrils as her chest rose from her rapid breathing. How a blush bloomed on her chest, and her lips parted ever so slightly.

No, she hadn't been scared.

She'd been intrigued.

As we approached the gate, tires crunched over the

gravel driveway, pulling our attention that way. Henley and Austin rode up on either side of me.

"What's she doing here?" Henley asked, adjusting his ball cap as he squinted that way. Fucker recognized her right away. Probably stared at her picture all fucking night.

"She's moving in." At least, that's what I assumed with her being here. I was glad to know she found my note I left in her gas pump with directions on how to get here. I hadn't had time to catch the guys up to speed. A ranch didn't run itself, and we all had our fair share of chores.

Austin's head swung my way. "You convinced her?"

Well, I'd mentioned it to Austin in passing in the barn earlier. Though, I'd only said we *may* have a guest for a while. He'd understood who I meant immediately.

I honestly hadn't thought she'd show up, but I guessed I was right about her. Her interest was piqued.

"Why didn't I know anything about this?" Henley questioned.

I sucked on my teeth. "You don't get information when you're the one who put us in this fucking mess in the first place. She wouldn't even be moving in if it wasn't for you."

"For me?" he asked, voice rising in pitch. "I didn't suggest you have the bitch move in with us."

"Watch your mouth, Henley," I warned, keeping my gaze on her car as she rolled to a stop. It was an old sedan. Easy to break into the trunk to fix the slashed tire. Chase clearly wasn't above petty games.

Austin held the gate open for us and we passed through, leaving him to close it behind us. We approached her car as she got out, immediately holding up a hand to shield her eyes from the sun as she looked up at us.

"So, you're cowboys," she said, tone flat.

"Ranchers," I corrected. "Henley here is the cowboy."

"Hey," he defended. "I do just as much as you two on that side of things."

Austin snorted.

"Where do I put my bags?" she asked, ignoring him and, stubbornly, me.

I turned Onyx around and said, "Henley, help her with her things."

I headed toward the barn and overheard Austin say, "My name's Austin, ma'am. Nice to meet you."

Boots landed in the dirt as Henley hopped off his horse, and a car door opened. To my surprise, Brynne's little footsteps followed me.

"I know their names," she said, catching up. "What's yours?"

I didn't respond as I eased Onyx to a stop outside the barn and dismounted.

"Seriously?" She propped a hand on her hip. The woman had an attitude, and it only made me want to mess with her more. See that little hip pop, those cheeks redden. "You break into my motel room, threaten me in an alley, and convince me to move in here, and I don't even get your name?"

"What'd I say the other night?"

She laughed, the sound dry, yet it pulled at me all the same. "I am *not* calling you Nightmare."

I shrugged. I didn't want her to, but it did me well seeing her irritated. "Then call me nothin'."

I looped the reins over Onyx's head, leading him into the barn, but she apparently wasn't done.

"Why'd you fix my tire?" she called behind me.

"Don't know what you're talking about," I said over my shoulder. I didn't need to admit that it was me who took the time to swap the tire. She could consider it a good deed from a bystander, for all I cared. I only did it so she had a way to get here, should she choose that route. If she hadn't, I probably would have just gone straight to the source to get the deed back. But now that she was here, I supposed I could have some fun.

"Sorry about him," Austin said from outside the barn door, his voice echoing down the aisle.

Ever the gentleman, that Austin. The girls fell for him left and right, and I wouldn't be surprised if Brynne landed in his trap. I couldn't care less if she did, but she wouldn't be staying on this ranch once we got the deed back. That was my only goal, and then all distractions would be gone.

Because I had a feeling if she stayed, she'd be nothing but trouble.

CHAPTER 6

BRYNNE

I thought the house looked grand from the outside, but the interior put it to shame. Rich brown leather covered every stool, chair, and sofa, with a massive rug taking up the entirety of the vaulted-ceiling living room. A larger-than-I-thought-possible TV was mounted on the wall, right below a moose head. Again, I didn't think the size of it was realistic.

"His dad's prized possession." Henley came down the stairs, still wearing that tan, felt cowboy hat, the brim higher on his forehead now. His close-cropped hair was nearly nonexistent under his hat, along with his striking green eyes. "Or, was," he corrected.

"He passed away?" I asked, noticing my bags were nowhere in sight.

Henley dipped his chin in a nod.

"I got to get back out there," he said, hooking his thumb over his shoulder in the direction of the front door.

"Which room is mine?"

He grabbed the handle, opening the heavy door. "Upstairs, last room on the left."

As soon as he shut it, the house was gratingly silent, my ears ringing.

Rather than head upstairs, I figured I'd look around to get accustomed to the place I'd be staying in for the foreseeable future. The house was void of all color aside from various shades of brown. No wonder the man was a grouch. He didn't know how to decorate.

The key to a happy mind was to surround yourself with things you loved, and the mood this house put me in told me enough.

I trailed my finger along a thin, long oak table, not a speck of dust to be found. So he was a neat freak, too.

At the end of the wide hallway was the kitchen. The dark oak cabinets and black granite countertops didn't surprise me one bit. Even the fridge was disguised with massive oak doors, blending in seamlessly.

On the opposite side of the kitchen sat what looked to be an office, and an idea sparked with the sight of paperwork sitting neatly atop the desk.

If he wouldn't tell me his name, I'd just have to figure it out myself.

Glancing out the large floor-to-ceiling windows, I saw the three of them still out by the barn, hosing the horses off. Surely, that'd keep them busy long enough for me to snoop.

The office had no doors, so I slipped in. At least if they did find me, I didn't have to explain why I'd gone in a closed room. It was wide open, practically inviting me in itself.

Tall mahogany bookshelves lined one side of the room,

and with a glance at the wide windows that spanned the other side, I crouched to try to keep myself hidden from view in case they looked this way. Making it to the desk, I scanned the script on the papers, but it was just a bunch of instruction manuals for various tools and appliances. I thumbed through the stack, finding nothing of use.

Opting to dig deeper rather than leave it be, I opened one of the drawers, shuffling through the files crammed inside. Each paper held tiny script, and my eyes strained to make out any names that might pop out to me as the words jumbled together.

Why didn't he want me to know his name?

Tiptoeing to the other side of the desk, I opened another drawer, finding dozens of files just like the other. My legs were falling asleep as I crouched, so I lowered my knees to the cowhide rug, flipping through folder after folder.

As I was just about to give up on the drawer, something pressed on my back, and against my better judgment, I let out a small shriek.

"What are you looking for?"

Just who I wanted to catch me. Why couldn't it be Austin or Henley?

I pushed the drawer shut, the soft-close slowing its dramatic effect. I silently cursed the fancy mechanics and stood, whirling on him.

"Oh, don't get off your knees for me, Darlin'. I quite liked you down there."

I rolled my eyes, crossing my arms over my breasts and popping a hip. "I'm looking for your name."

He took off his black cowboy hat, setting it upside

down on the desk beside me. "Won't find it in here. Or anywhere in this house, in fact."

I tried to keep my eyes from taking in his entire face and the allure he held based on looks alone. The mask and the hat last night had been...shockingly enticing, but this man, with his close cropped hair and dark, full beard drew me in, and that in itself was dangerous. "Why's that?"

He invaded my space, dark eyes pinned to mine. "Because I cover my tracks, Brynne, and I think you should start doing the same once we're done with you."

Done with me? As if they were using me like a tissue, only to be thrown away when the job was done. The fact that he hid himself so well, even within his own home, piqued my interest. What did he have to hide?

"What do you want with my ex?"

He grabbed his hat, walking over to the rack by the entry of the office to set it on a hook. "Get some sleep. We can chat through all your little questions in the morning."

I glanced out the windows, the sun just barely setting. "It's not even dark."

He ignored me, making it clear he didn't give a shit. What he really wanted to say was *get the fuck out of my office*, and I had to be thankful he didn't phrase it that way. He crossed back to the desk, stepping around the edge to pull out the chair. He took a seat, taking his laptop out of the small drawer under the wood top.

"I want to talk about it *now*. I'm staying in your fucking house."

His lips thinned as he looked at me. "I don't give a shit what you want to do. This is my house, and I want to be alone, so get the fuck out of my office."

Ah, there it was.

He opened his laptop as I asked, simply to get under his skin, "How can you ever be alone with two other guys under the same roof?"

He typed on the keyboard, not bothering to look my way anymore. "Their company is much more enjoyable than yours. They know a little something about personal space."

My mouth popped open as anger pulsed through me. Was he fucking kidding? If anyone needed to be educated on space, it was *him.*

As his fingers moved, the screen lighting up his face, I wanted to keep digging. Or bait him to slip up. Either worked. But by his posture alone, I knew I wasn't going to get anything out of him. Though I hated the satisfaction he must have felt in getting his way, I turned and left the office, walking back through the kitchen to head up the stairs, finding my room easily. Rather than going to sleep, though, I threw on a pair of leggings and a sports bra and headed outside for a run.

Nothing made me feel better than a long stretch of cardio and the pounding of my heart. It was simply a plus that the view was spectacular on this ranch. To my displeasure, I had the nightmare of a man inside to thank for that. Otherwise, I never would have been fortunate enough to have this view on one of my runs.

I guessed things weren't as bad as they initially seemed. Or at least, I hoped.

My stay on this ranch was still young.

CHAPTER 7

BOOKER

From the window in my office, I had the perfect view of Brynne jogging up and down the driveway last night. I was sure she knew I could see her, her tan belly on display in only a sports bra and high-waisted leggings that crossed in the front. She knew exactly what she was doing, and yet, I couldn't look away.

Her ponytail had brushed over her shoulders each time it swung back and forth, sweat dripping down her skin, mouth parted as she breathed deeply. I wanted to see her like that, but in an entirely different setting. All her workout managed to do was get my cock hard, which turned into a hot shower with my fist pumping to relieve myself.

With a hand on the glass to keep myself up, I'd watched my release wash down the drain, figuring it was better than all over her back, but not nearly as heavenly feeling. Throughout the night, I'd kept my ears open to listen for Austin or Henley in case they got any bright ideas and snuck into her room. Last thing I needed was Henley causing more problems that I had to clean up.

I pulled on a black t-shirt and dark wash jeans, then headed downstairs, eager for a quick breakfast and to get outside. Nothing took a fraction of the stress off my shoulders like fresh air and silence, save for the sounds of nature. But as I descended the last step, I knew my wishes wouldn't be coming true today.

Brynne stood by the kitchen island with her arms crossed as Henley and Austin dug into an egg scramble, their coffees steaming from their mugs.

"We need to talk," Brynne said, popping that hip of hers.

Walking past her, I opened the cabinet to pull out my own mug, then poured a cup of coffee, all while she stared at me. Women always caused shit so fucking early.

"Whatcha want to talk about?" Austin asked after swallowing his bite.

She held her hands out, brows raised. "Why the fuck I'm here, for a start."

Henley opened his mouth to respond, but I shot him a warning glare. I didn't need the man blabbing his mouth and telling her too much. For all we knew, she was just as eager to take this ranch, or willing to be on Chase's side, regardless of his treatment of her in the alley. Whether he handled her like that on the regular or not, she might be too attached to him to give a shit.

"Sit," I instructed, crossing my arms.

She didn't.

With a long exhale, my thumb and forefinger pinched

the bridge of my nose. This woman was going to give me a headache for the entirety of her stay.

I leaned back against the counter, setting my mug beside me as I faced her. "Your boyfriend has something of ours."

"*Ex*-boyfriend," she corrected. "What is it?"

"That's not for you to know," I answered. She didn't need to know the logistics. She just had to cooperate and be our bait.

The corners of her mouth turned down as she shrugged, dropping her arms. "Okay." She walked out of the kitchen, disappearing from sight for a moment before reappearing with a bag. *Her* bag. "I'll just be going, then."

How did I know she wouldn't let this go that easily?

Another sigh escaped my lips, and I had a feeling I'd be doing that a lot for the next week or so. "Put the bag down."

She held it between her legs, both hands on the strap. "Only if you're honest with me."

"You don't need to know the details of why you're here."

Austin's and Henley's eyes darted between us as they continued to eat. This was a fucking joke to them. I was really standing here arguing with a woman I'd just met. A woman I had no interest in fighting for. Any other girl, I'd have sent her to the curb by now. I didn't have time for attitude, and yet here she stood, full of it, and I was only encouraging the behavior. I should bend her over a fucking chair and spank her till her ass was red just to teach her a little lesson, my handprint the only thing she could feel.

She kept those hard eyes on me, determination shining bright as all get out. I mentally shook my head. She'd probably fucking like it. "I say I do, so either tell me or I'm leaving."

I crossed the kitchen, invading her space. "And where are you going to go. Huh? Crying back to Chase?"

Her lips thinned, and I could tell I'd gotten under her skin. "I have friends."

"Then why were you at a motel? Why not their place?"

Her nostrils flared the slightest bit. "Because I left him late at night." Her words were a tad softer, and for some fucking reason, I felt an inkling of guilt. My stomach soured at the idea of feeling even an ounce of remorse.

"Not a smart move, then. Which is exactly why you don't need to know what he took." I put a finger under her chin, tilting my head the slightest bit. "Just keep looking like a sad little damsel, and you'll do just fine."

She smacked my hand away, her cheeks turning a hint of pink. "I am *not* a fucking damsel in distress. In case you didn't notice, I was doing just fine before you broke into my motel room, and when you pinned me in a fucking alley."

"You did what?" Austin asked from behind us, but I didn't pay him any mind.

Our chests touched as I narrowed my eyes. "Oh, is that right?"

"Mhmm," she hummed.

"That why you had to walk to that shithole because you couldn't fix your tire? Or why you were a sitting duck with the receptionist giving your key out like fucking candy to whatever horny shithead walked into that joint?" I backed her up until she hit the wall, and I fought not to wrap my hand around her delicate little throat. My palm practically tingled with the memory of it. "You'll have much more fun sitting vulnerable in my house, Darlin'. Let me remind you that you agreed to come here. You're under my roof, and once you're in, you're fucking in. I don't let my targets go easy, so if you want to run, run. But I'll find you. And you'll regret your feet ever hit the ground."

Her jaw was clenched, her gaze unwavering as she leveled me. I'd let her be determined, let her think she had an inkling of control here, but I was in charge, and she'd listen.

A throat cleared behind me, and Henley, the blabber-mouth that he was, said, "I lost the deed to the ranch in a bet with your ex."

I bit my bottom lip so hard, I swore my teeth almost cut it clean off. Brynne fucking smiled at me, then squeezed out from between my body and the wall, walking over to the boys.

"Thanks so much, Hen," she said, her voice all sweet and seductive.

Fuck her, and fuck Henley.

She leaned her elbows on the island, opposite Henley and Austin, popping her ass out. My eyes betrayed me, sticking to her plump ass like glue.

"So, you're going to what? Lose the ranch?" she asked, pressing her arms together the slightest bit to put her cleavage on display. She knew exactly what the fuck she was doing.

Henley nodded as Austin looked to me for help.

Henley couldn't give a fuck less about the consequences, but Austin was stuck between a rock and a hard place.

She chewed on her lip, thinking. "And you want me to lure him here to what...? Get it back?"

Henley shrugged. "Or kill him."

Austin pasted on a large, fake smile as he set a hand on Henley's shoulder. "You see, Henley here is a little imaginative. What he means is to scare him a bit."

Henley's mouth pulled to one side as he thought of that as an option, as if it wasn't before. "Yeah, or kill him. Whatever it comes down to."

He was fucking admitting that he wanted to murder someone right in front of a woman who could easily go report him, and then we'd all be screwed.

"Henley," I barked, approaching the island. "Shut your mouth."

Brynne's brows rose, as if my words really shocked her. We both knew they didn't. "Still mad at him, Nightmare?"

The way she used the nickname, that I'd intended as a joke, pissed me off. "Henley's fine. It's you I can't stand."

She straightened, popping her chest out the slightest bit. "Is that so?"

I gave her a bored stare. "Yep."

"Then why invite me into your home?"

"I've already told you—"

She cut me off. "There's other ways to get the deed from him."

I stepped a foot closer to her. "Maybe I just wanted to have some fun in the meantime."

She glared at me, then looked back to Austin and Henley. "What's the plan?"

Austin and Henley exchanged looks, then turned to me. "You lure him here," I answered.

"He'll think it's a setup," she replied, not facing me. "There's no reason I'd be on a ranch in the middle of nowhere."

Austin shoved his plate forward so he could fold his hands together on the granite. "So we give him a few days to forget."

Brynne arched a brow. "How are you so sure he'll forget about the ranch that easily? I'm sure he's eager to turn in the papers and take over ownership."

"I've done business with him before," Henley said. "He's lazy and has to report all his earnings to his boss. I'm sure he's not too eager to do that so quickly, so if I had to guess, he'll hold on to it for a while."

Brynne's cheek moved as she presumably chewed on it in thought. "Okay. We wait a week, lure him here, then I'm free to go?"

I nodded. "You'll be free to do whatever the fuck you want after."

She sent me the fakest, sweetest look. "How nice of you."

"Have to do chores to earn your keep, though," I said.

Her mouth popped open. "You invited me."

"Only if you want to do them," Austin piped in, leaning forward on his stool slightly.

I kept my stare on Brynne. "She's doing them."

Her eyes lit up like an idea hit her, and I internally groaned. "Fine. I'll do them if you tell me your name."

I shook my head. "You don't need my name to feed horses and scoop shit."

She shrugged, glancing at her nails. "You're right. But I just won't cooperate until you tell me."

I wouldn't budge, and she must've seen it in my stance, because she added, "If I'm going to trust you, then you have to trust me, and that includes you telling me your name."

I crossed my arms, giving a tight nod in her direction. "Then beg, Darlin'."

CHAPTER 8

BRYNNE

I spun on him. "Excuse me?" The man was crazy if he thought I'd be at his mercy that easily.

"You heard what I said." His gaze darkened as a sort of hunger crept into those midnight eyes. "I'll only tell you my name if you're a good little slut and beg for it."

My eyes were practically slits as I mentally threw daggers at him. He was an asshole, the biggest prick I'd ever met, and yet, a part of me wanted to be on my knees before him, at his command. I also wanted to see the utter shock on his face if I did, and the thrill of his rough voice shot sparks through me. Chase had never told me what to do, let alone ever called me a slut. I almost hated that I liked it.

What did I have to lose?

I lowered myself until my knees hit the hard ground, all the while keeping my eyes glued to his. To my disappointment, his expression didn't change at all. He still looked bored as all get out. From this side of the counter, Austin and Henley couldn't see me down here, save for probably the top of my head.

"Please, Nightmare, tell me your name so I can stop using this ridiculous nickname for you."

That got a reaction. The corners of his mouth tilted down the slightest bit behind his facial hair, annoyance ringing clear in his expression. Satisfaction made my lips curl up.

He roughly grabbed my chin, tilting my head further back as he bent the slightest bit. "I'd be careful mouthing off while you're on your knees before me. Never know what I'll fill this little mouth with to make you shut up."

I kept my jaw set, determined not to let his words get to me. Though it seemed they had the opposite effect of offending me as heat pooled in my core.

"Maybe I should fuck that stubborn little tongue clean, huh?" He leaned closer, his voice lowering. "Does that make you wet, Darlin'?"

Again, I kept quiet. I wouldn't give him the satisfaction of knowing he'd gotten what he wanted. My panties were already soaked.

"Where do you draw the line?" he asked, the set of his brow softening a bit.

"What?"

"What am I allowed to do to you?"

Realization hit me. He actually wanted to do this. It wasn't an act—he truly liked me at his mercy, and he intended to play.

"Anything." The word came out in a whisper, eliciting a small chuckle from him.

"I didn't hear you."

"You can do anything to me," I said, finding my voice.

He arched a thick brow. "That's a big answer."

Stubbornly, I simply glared back. If he thought I couldn't take whatever he doled out, he highly underestimated me. "You don't think I can take it?"

He straightened, keeping my chin in between his fingers. "Maybe. But even with your confidence, you need to pick a safe word."

"Who says you don't need one, too?"

From the other side of the island, I heard a low whistle come from one of the guys.

The man before me chuckled again, pity in the sound. "Darlin', it's you I'm worried about."

"Fine. Horse." It was the first word that came to mind, but it didn't matter what it was. I wouldn't be using it.

He let me go. "You bring any toys?"

I blinked, the question taking me off guard. I nodded in response.

"Go get 'em, then."

Using the counter to pull myself up, I didn't glance at Austin or Henley as I walked out of the kitchen and went up the stairs. Once I was in the room I was staying in, I rifled through my luggage until I found my favorite vibrator. It was small, but the bullet had a lot of power, coming with multiple settings.

I made my way back downstairs, the vibrator gripped in my hand. When I reentered the kitchen, Austin and Henley were gone.

"Where'd they go?" I asked the guy where he still stood, but now he was leaning against the island.

"Wouldn't want them to hear you, would you?"

I didn't answer. Honestly, I didn't think I'd mind, but

something about this man told me he wouldn't want to share.

"On your knees," he commanded.

I started to lower back to the ground, but he shook his head, lifting his chin to the spot in front of him. "Right here."

I walked over to him, slowly lowering myself back to the ground. The cold tile bit through my leggings to my knees, but it did nothing to cool the heat casting over every inch of my skin. This man was a stranger, someone I'd just barely met, and I didn't even know his name. Yet, I was practically dripping through my leggings at the thrill of what might happen. I was single now, with no obligation to anyone. I could've said no, rejected the man in front of me, but my entire life had been a series of no's. Today, it'd be yes.

He held his palm out, calluses littering his skin, and I set the toy in his hand. He knew exactly what he was doing as he clicked it on, the vibrator buzzing to life.

"What was it that you wanted from me?" he asked, knowing damn well what the answer was.

I adjusted my arms, pushing my boobs out a bit more so my v-neck showcased my cleavage. "Your name."

He twisted the vibrator in his fingers, watching me. "And what did I say you had to do?"

"Beg."

"And what aren't you doing?"

My nostrils flared the slightest bit. It was obvious he wasn't going to make this easy.

I leaned forward slightly. The bulge in his jeans was massive as it pressed up against the dark denim. Rather than using my hand, I stuck my tongue out, trailing it up the fabric. He stared down at me, our eyes locked as heat flickered in his gaze. Once I hit the top of the zipper, the tip of my tongue flicking past the button, I said, "Please tell me your name."

He stared at me, likely judging if he should give in that easily, but of course, he was making me work for it. "Tongue out, Darlin'."

I did, sticking it out as far as it would go. He clicked the vibrator up a speed, then pressed the silicone tip to my tongue. It tickled slightly, making my senses go on high alert.

He dragged it from the tip to the back, nearly hitting my gag reflex but stopping short, then brought it back to the tip. A few more passes, and he pulled it away, holding it in front of me. "Spit on it."

I raised up a bit, letting my spit drip onto the toy.

Once it was covered to his liking, he knelt so we were eye level. Keeping his gaze locked on mine, he used his free hand to pull the top of my leggings away from my belly, then stuck his other hand with the vibrator inside. He easily pulled my panties away, situating the toy directly over my clit. Instantly, my body buzzed to life, ecstasy rippling through me. It took every ounce of control to keep the blissful sensation from showing.

He dipped one finger inside me, coating his skin, then removed his hand, leaving the toy in my panties. He let my leggings fling back against my belly, my body flinching slightly as it pulled the vibrator firmer to my clit.

"Open your mouth."

My lips parted, and he slid his glistening finger inside, pressing it down against my tongue.

"I don't feel very convinced that I should tell you my name," he said, hooking his thumb under my chin. "I think you're doing just fine without it."

"Please," I mumbled around his finger, and then I closed my lips around the digit, sucking hard. The flavor of me coated my tongue, and I swallowed as he used his thumb to pull my face closer to his. His other hand drifted down, clicking up the speed on the toy through my leggings, causing electricity to flow through me as my legs strained to keep up.

"You're fucking soaked. Such a dirty little slut, aren't you?"

I nodded as a small noise escaped my throat.

"You like this, don't you? Being on your knees before a stranger, so willing to let me use you."

I hummed my response as he cupped the vibrator through the fabric of my pants, pressing it harder to my clit.

"If you come, you don't get my name," he warned, and I nearly wept at the thought of not letting myself give in to the pleasure that coursed through every inch of my body. "You can wait until I let you, can't you?"

I blinked rapidly, trying to rein in my impending orgasm. I was almost willing to let myself go, damn his name.

He pressed the button through my leggings again, all while keeping his finger in my mouth, upping the speed.

He shoved his finger deeper, tightening his thumb under my chin. I choked slightly, my eyes watering the smallest bit. With the act, he slowly withdrew his finger, trailing it over my cheek and down my neck.

"What's the magic word, Brynne?"

"Please," I panted, my voice desperate, as I could barely hold my orgasm back any longer. "Please tell me your name."

He could tell I was close, teetering on the edge as I fought to keep it at bay. Just when I thought I couldn't hold it back any longer, he said, "You can come."

I dropped the pathetic hold I had on myself and let the pleasure rip through me. I nearly collapsed, thinking I could hold myself up on my own, but then I set a hand out on his shoulder as I dipped my head, and he grabbed my arm to hold me up, keeping me upright on my knees.

I let out a moan, my mouth wide open as I tried to keep my noises quiet. I didn't know where Austin and Henley were, but it wasn't like it was a secret what was happening in here.

The vibrator was still stuck to my clit, waves of pleasure rumbling through me as it continued eliciting pleasure, despite the fact that I already came.

I went to take it out, but he grabbed my hand, shaking his head. "I want one more out of you."

But with his words alone, my hand still gripped in the fabric of his shirt, another wave of pleasure came all on its own. I screamed out, pressing the top of my head to his chest as he let me use him for support while my second orgasm ripped through me. With my vibrator alone, I'd never had such a powerful feeling ripple through my entire body, and I didn't know if I could take any more.

I tried to swallow through my heavy breathing, and he brought a hand up to my hair, resting it on my neck. "Take it out."

I released one of my hands from him, slipping it into my pants to pull the toy out. The entire vibrator was soaked in my cum, my body shaking from release. I turned it off, setting it on the ground as I caught my breath. Once I was composed enough, I pulled away from him.

He gave me one last look, and I almost hated the softness that appeared for the first time since I'd met him.

He stood, moving to grab his coffee mug from the counter. I stayed on the floor, looking up at him expectantly.

After a long sip, he stared out the window, almost like I wasn't there. But then, when I thought he wouldn't say a word, he muttered, "Booker."

And left.

CHAPTER 9

BRYNNE

As to be expected, the diner was slow. A couple was seated in the far corner by the window, and our usual customer sat at the bar. Outside, fog clouded the streets, making visibility poor enough that you could barely see the road through the glass. Though it was midday, the street lights were on in an unsuccessful attempt to lighten the stagnant gray clouds. All the lampposts did was create an eerie glow through the mist, the light not touching the ground.

McKenna popped her bubblegum next to me as I stood lost in thought behind the counter, thinking of what I did in front of Booker yesterday. He'd barely looked at me and popped a vibrator on my clit and I came undone. I didn't think I'd been so turned on before in my life, and it was all due to the way his gaze devoured me.

His eyes held control in a way I'd never seen before, and images of him wearing the half skeleton mask flashed in my mind. Even covering himself, he commanded a room. Hell, he could probably order an entire town around hidden behind that mask, and they'd not think twice about obeying.

And when he'd told me not to come…my body had no choice but to heed his demand. Then, when I'd gone up to my room, I'd tested his name on my lips and came again just to the memory of his eyes alone. The way he had this much power over me so soon after meeting him was dangerous, if not reckless.

Chase never had that effect on me. He was all dark blonde hair, blue eyes, and well-manicured hands. Booker was rough in every aspect of the word. With his voice, the set of his brows, the way he held himself. When he'd slipped that vibrator over my clit, he knew exactly where to set it, and the knowledge that he knew his way around a woman like that—well, the thought alone built heat between my legs where I stood, causing me to adjust my stance in order to hide the thoughts that were swirling through my mind.

"You're not at the motel anymore, then, right?" McKenna asked, twirling her finger around the end of her blonde ponytail.

I'd told her the gist of what transpired over the last seventy-two hours, but with a few interruptions, I'd left some details out. "Nope."

She wagged her eyebrows at me, a hip propped against the silver edge of the counter. "So you're saying you're in *his* room, then."

My mouth popped open as I fought my body's natural reaction to blush. "No fucking way."

She set a hand on the speckled counter. "I saw them! The one you said…"

She searched her memory for his name, so I filled in the blank. "Booker."

"Booker!" She slapped her hand on the flat surface. "And his friend. They were cute! It wouldn't be *that* bad to land in bed with at least one of them."

I grabbed a rag from behind the bar, along with a spray bottle filled with anti-bacterial solution. "It would be bad."

I spritzed the counter, then wiped in circular motions.

A gasp escaped McKenna's mouth and I cringed.

"You already slept with him!" she blurted.

I widened my eyes, shooting her a look that screamed *shut up*. "I did not," I whisper-shouted back.

Doug, one of our regulars, adjusted his newspaper, not bothering to look at the two of us where we gossiped not three feet from him. "She definitely did."

McKenna pointed a finger his way. "See. Even he can tell."

I kept scrubbing, like that'd make her stop talking about it. It wouldn't. McKenna would keep nagging me until she knew the full truth, and even then, she'd want to know more.

I stepped closer to her, mumbling, "Okay. Fine. He made me...you know."

Her chewing jaw ceased for a moment as she thought on that. "He made you orgasm?!"

The whole fucking diner turned our way.

Doug, the poor sap that he was, peered over the paper, his reading glasses low on his nose.

I grabbed McKenna's arm, pulling her through the swinging door to the kitchen. I whirled on her. "You can't just announce that!"

But she didn't care. Not with that beaming smile spreading her lips wider than I'd ever seen before. "Was he good?"

"We didn't sleep together," I said in a hushed, hurried tone.

"Wait, so he went down on you?"

I shook my head, but before I could answer her, a pissed off voice yelled from the front, "Where the fuck is Brynne Hansley?"

Our eyes widened as we moved to peer through the circular window. Instantly, I knew it wasn't Booker or Chase. Whoever it was, they were pissed, and if I had to guess by the use of my name, that anger was aimed towards me.

I had half a mind not to go back through the door, but then the bull of a man grabbed Doug by the collar of his shirt, lifting him out of his seat. "I said where the fuck is she?!"

McKenna tried to grab my arm, knowing damn well that announcing I was here wouldn't end well, but I had no choice. The man seemed like he would tear this place apart brick by brick until he found me.

I shoved through the door, evading her grasp, and said, "Right here."

The man was a lot more intimidating on this side of the window, and I instantly regretted my decision. There was no going back now. Not as he tossed Doug aside like a piece of meat, then jumped over the counter, closing in on me. I didn't move. If I did, I'd look scared, but quite frankly, I was fucking petrified.

His unsettling gaze roamed over my body, head to toe,

before his face was in mine. He had a good foot and a half on me at least, but he crouched, which somehow made him all the more intimidating. That, and his bald head and full beard.

"Where'd your little boyfriend run off to, skank?"

The insult made me want to coil in on myself.

"He's not my boyfriend."

But bull man didn't give a shit. He grabbed my shirt in both fists, shoving me back so that the edge of the counter dug into my lower back. The awkward angle in which he held me hurt like hell, but again, I refused to show it.

"You want to keep lying now?"

McKenna moved like she wanted to step in, but he'd just toss her aside like he did Doug, and I didn't want my best friend getting hurt because of this pig. Subtle enough so he wouldn't see, I sent her a slight hand gesture to stay put.

"I'm not lying. If he isn't at his house, then I have no clue where he is."

His fists tightened, his jaw clenching. "Don't play the little innocent act. I see right the fuck through it."

"Then you must need your eyes checked, because there's nothing to see through."

I probably shouldn't have said that, because next thing I knew, my body was shoved harder against the counter, pain surging up my back.

"Next time, you better know where he is. Otherwise, I'll take you as his payment."

He dropped me to the ground, my feet hitting the linoleum with a thud. Rather than jumping back over like before, he walked around the bar, leaving the diner.

McKenna was next to me in an instant, her hand on my arm. "Who the fuck was that?"

One of my hands rubbed at my chest, the other on my lower back. "No idea, and I don't care to find out."

Her fingers shook slightly, and I felt terrible for it. "What if he comes back?"

"He won't," I said. "And if he does, he'll figure out soon enough that I have no information to give him."

But he'd given me intel he didn't know I benefited from.

The couple from the booth had darted out as soon as the man jumped the counter, but Doug remained, staring at us from where he stood. "You ladies alright?"

I nodded. "Fine. Thanks, Doug. Sorry he took things out on you."

He waved me off, grabbing his newspaper and folding it into a neat rectangle. "It takes a lot more than that to rattle me. But whatever he wants, he's motivated. I'd be careful if I was the two of you."

With a swallow, I said, "We will."

At least, as best we could.

———

Booker, Henley, and Austin were nowhere to be found when I'd gotten back to the ranch after my shift, so I'd headed upstairs, hiding away in my room. I was fully content with spending the rest of the night in this bed. The mattress was softer than any other I'd slept in before, the comforter like a giant cloud against the lingering pain in my lower back. There was no better way to be wrapped than in the comfort of these blankets, and I hoped like hell none of them would check on me. Not that they would, anyway. I meant nothing to them. I was here for one purpose, and that was to get them their deed back. The information I now had could wait until tomorrow when I wasn't so shaken up.

I hated even thinking the words, knowing that I'd let that guy get to me. Rattling me was his every intention, and he'd been successful. Giving him that satisfaction, even if he didn't know it right now, filled me with disappointment and rage. Both feelings were aimed towards myself— knowing that I was so weak for letting my mind dwell on what happened for this long.

With the white comforter pulled up to my chin and my head buried in a pillow, I heard the door softly open. If the house hadn't already been silent, I wouldn't have known, but who stood in the entry to the room was all too obvious as Booker's presence filled the space.

"Almost thought you packed up and left," Booker said, his voice coming from the doorway.

"Nope." My voice was muffled by the comfy cloud enveloping me.

Silence stuck to the air like tape on paper, and I almost thought he may have left, but then he spoke again. "Good day at work?"

I stared at the creamy pillow case with what little light wafted into the room from the open door. The sun had already set by the time I got home, and I hadn't bothered to turn on any lights or change my clothes before crawling into bed.

"It was fine," I replied blandly.

Even if it wasn't, what did he care? Why was he standing there trying to make small talk as if this was some kind of friendship? Or relationship, even. It was none of that. We were hardly acquaintances, and from the few impressions I had of Booker, he didn't seem like a chatty guy.

Boots stomped on the hardwood, turning muffled as they passed onto the rug, then the comforter was yanked off the bed, exposing me.

"Hey!" I yelled, sitting up.

"What the fuck are you doing?" he grumbled.

"I should be asking you that!"

His furious eyes took in my uniform. "You're wearing fucking work clothes in bed and moping like a wet fucking cat. What the fuck happened?"

"Nothing fucking happened," I shot back, getting up on my knees to lean over the edge of the bed in an attempt to grab the blanket.

Before I could grasp the fabric, an arm looped around my waist, and I was tossed back at the pillows, bouncing slightly on the mattress.

"What the fuck, Booker!"

His lips were pressed into a firm line. "Talk."

"There's nothing to talk about," I said, digging my fingers into the pillow. My skirt had risen up my thighs, and I was well aware he could see my underwear with my legs bent up to my chest.

"This ain't fucking high school, Darlin'." He leaned closer, grabbing the edge of my skirt and yanking it toward himself. "Now put on your fucking big girl panties and tell me why you're laying in this bed like you'd rather it be a coffin."

Sheesh. And he thought I was dramatic?

"Chase still has the deed."

Booker froze, then a second later, his brows pulled inward. "How do you know that?"

"I just do."

He pulled the fabric harder, and I swore it'd tear. "You go see him today? Huh, Brynne?" Then, his voice dropped, and our mouths were inches apart. "Your little orgasm yesterday not enough for your needy little pussy?"

I had to press my lips together in order to stop the tremble that threatened to show. I couldn't let him see how he got under my skin. "One of his friends visited me at work." He didn't need to know the guy probably wasn't a *friend* of Chase's.

A pulse ticked in his jaw. "What do you mean, visited?"

I supposed there was no point in trying to lie now. "Visited, as in he jumped over the counter and grabbed me. Told me I'd be his payment if Chase didn't hand it over."

Booker's eyes flashed, violence so potent swirling in the depths of his irises. "Where did he touch you."

My breathing was almost nonexistent as I slowly brought my hand up to the collar of my shirt.

He didn't look at the placement, but he knew. "What did he do."

I swallowed the rock threatening to choke me. "He shoved me against the counter." The words were quiet, full of breath.

His jaw moved as he ground his teeth together, the movement the only sound in the room as my lungs ceased to work. That look on his face—it was one I never wanted aimed towards me.

He let go of my skirt and stepped away from the bed, not meeting my gaze. "You've got chores tonight, so get dressed and out to the barn."

Then he left, taking all the oxygen in the room with him.

I had a feeling I'd need to get used to him leaving.

CHAPTER 10

BRYNNE

Crickets chirped out in the fields as bugs darted around the spotlight above the barn. Austin had given me a quick rundown of how to feed the horses, then he'd disappeared inside the house, muttering something about needing a stiff drink after the day he'd had. Working on a ranch day in and day out had to be hard, but I could tell the three of them loved it. I wasn't sure if anyone else helped them or not, but they seemed to have things under control—not that I knew anything about ranching, though.

I used the pocket knife sitting on one of the bales to cut the bailing twine, then set it on a shelf so it didn't get lost in the mess of hay. I filled the wheelbarrow to its max, then headed down the aisle, tossing a flake in for each horse. The barn had to be twice as long as the house, holding about twenty-five stalls. Only ten of them were occupied, the others out in the pasture.

After I finished feeding the horses in the barn, I refilled the wheelbarrow and headed outside. Over a dozen horses waited by the fence, making various noises as they awaited their dinner. Unlatching the gate, I squeezed inside with the wheelbarrow, making sure to close it behind me. The horses swarmed, but I pushed it about ten feet in, then started tossing the flakes around, spacing them about two to three feet apart, like Austin had instructed.

I grabbed the wheelbarrow, but right as I did, a clang rang out, like a chain hitting the fence. I looked over my shoulder, searching the pitch black field for any signs of an animal or person, but it was quiet again. My mind was most likely still reeling from the man at the diner. There was nothing out here besides a few livestock animals.

Leaving the horses to eat their hay, I slipped back out the gate, making sure it was latched properly, then pushed the wheelbarrow back to the barn. The wheel crunched over the loose rocks in the dirt, then went silent as it moved onto smooth concrete inside the barn.

I wheeled it back to where I found it, then flicked the floodlight off on my way out. Once the beam disappeared, that same clanking sound came from the field, and I whirled, squinting my eyes in an attempt to see better. Only pure black stared back at me, which was expected.

"Just the wind, Brynne. Calm down," I muttered to myself, continuing on my way toward the house.

But then the sound came again, and I froze. My heart beat in my ears, and even the crickets paused their song.

I wasn't alone.

"Hello?" I called into the void.

I should keep going. Get into the house and lock the door.

Footsteps on dirt sounded, and then my eyes focused in

on a body by the barn. In the dim light from the moon, I recognized the mask before anything else.

My body should have relaxed even a fraction, but every nerve stayed on high alert, fear overtaking my senses in a rush.

His hand moved, a glint of light reflecting off whatever he held, and then the clang sounded again as he hit the object against the hitching post.

"You can run from your fear, Brynne. But if I catch you, I have my way." Even from where I stood, I heard him loud and clear.

"What are you going to do to me?" I hated the uncertainty in my voice. I wasn't sure what he was trying to do, or why my body was lit bright like a sparkler at the idea.

He casually prowled forward, the item in his hand jingling with every step. "Would you like to find out?"

I swallowed. Did I? I should say no. Go inside and lie back in that heaven of a bed. But a part of me wanted to know. Wanted to experience firsthand what he'd do to me if he got his hands on me again. If it was anything like the first time, I had no reason to object.

"Maybe," I answered, realizing how stupid my response sounded.

"Then run, Darlin'."

I hesitated, which wasn't the smartest move, because he was already running, and I was still frozen in place. I spun, darting in the direction of the house, but he was taller, faster, and was gaining fast. My shoes pounded on the gravel as I booked it toward the corner of the house, speeding around the side. One glance over my shoulder told me I had no hope of getting away, but I could try. My chest heaved, my heart pounding dangerously as I made it behind the house. But then, Booker's boots sounded directly behind me, and I screamed.

Large arms wrapped around my waist, and I was lifted from the ground mere feet from the first step of the porch. We were both breathing heavily, but for different reasons. His was from sprinting to catch me, and mine was from the anticipation of what was to come.

He threw me over his shoulder, landing a slap to my ass through my loose shorts, then hauled me back to the barn, not bothering to turn the light on as we entered. The slight sting sent a surge of heat through my core, and I silently wanted his hand on me again. He carried me like I was barely more than a paper weight, an attestation to the muscles toning his arms. His hand wrapped around a bundle of bailing twine, and then he set me down, pinning me between his body and a stall.

He grabbed my hands, forcing them together, and wrapped the twine around them multiple times, tying the ends in a knot. The frayed string bit into the soft skin of my wrists, but I barely felt it as he lifted my arms above my head, hooking the string on a metal hook above me. With the position, I was forced to keep my arms up. My thighs clenched together as I swore heat dripped from me.

Between the dark of night, his mask, and the black cowboy hat, I could barely see him, but it only fueled my fear and excitement more. His hands gripped the top of my baggy t-shirt and pulled down. The fabric tore easily, straight down the middle. I wasn't wearing a bra, assuming I would be going to sleep after I finished feeding the horses, and even with the low visibility, I could tell my exposed breasts made him feral.

"You didn't run very fast, Brynne," he said, seduction and hunger caressing every word that rolled off his tongue.

His finger hooked in the band of my shorts, and in seconds, they were pooled at my ankles. I only wore my light purple underwear now, and he was staring straight at them.

"Why is that?" he asked. "Did you want to be caught?" He came closer, to the point my nipples brushed his black t-shirt. The slight friction sent flickers of flames through my body. "Did you want me to have my way with this pretty little body of yours?"

I could only breathe, and I pushed my chest out further, aching for my breasts to press against his body.

With my silence, he grabbed one of my nipples between his thumb and pointer finger, pinching slightly. "Answer me."

"Yes," I whispered.

I didn't have to see his face to know he had the slightest smirk pulling at his mouth. He wanted me at his mercy, and I was here willingly.

He released my nipple, tearing my shirt off the rest of the way and tossing it to the ground. He unbuckled something from his belt loop, the object clinking.

"You remember our safe word?" he asked, voice low as he situated the strap on whatever he held.

"Yes."

"Good." Then, he brought his hand forward, and tiny pinpricks of pain needled my skin, right over my left breast, and my breath hitched.

He was trailing a spur along my bare skin.

He brought the rowel down, the spiked edges coasting over my nipple. A small moan escaped my lips, and he brought it back over the peaked bud.

"You like that, don't you, dirty little slut?"

I nodded, biting down on my lip as he trailed it over to the opposite breast. Every tiny spike that bit into my skin made my clit throb, and I wanted so bad to reach between my legs as he had his way with me.

He brought the spur lower, gliding it along my belly. The sensitive part, between my belly button and my pussy, jumped as he drew a figure eight in my skin. His other hand came up to my breast, gripping it just hard enough to where it felt blissful, as he brought the spur lower. He dragged it right along my clit, over the fabric of my panties, and I moaned again, my head falling back.

"Such a needy thing." He pinched my nipple between his fingers, rolling the rowel up and down, right over my swollen clit. He applied just the right amount of pressure, and I never wanted it to stop.

Bringing the spur back up, he circled my opposite nipple with it, gliding it over the bud every few passes. "Please don't stop."

His other hand gripped my breast even harder. "You're fucking begging for it, Darlin'. That's a dangerous thing."

"I don't care." My voice was more breath than anything.

"You should."

He tossed the spur to the ground, releasing my breast, then grabbed my hips, spinning me around so that I was facing the stall. My arms twisted as the twine stayed perched on the hook above me.

His hand smoothed over my ass before a crack split through the silence of the barn, his hand leaving a delicious sting on my skin.

"You want to be fucked like a bad little slut, don't you?"

I hummed my response, perking my ass higher. "I'm on birth control."

His hand gripped my waist, fingers digging into my skin. Then, he glided his rough palm along my ass, sliding a finger past my hole over my underwear to slide the material aside, sinking the digit into my soaking pussy.

"Fuck, Brynne," he hissed. "You fucking love this."

There was no hiding it. I wanted him inside me more than I thought possible.

He yanked my panties down my legs, letting them sit around my ankles along with my shorts. Then, I heard him pull down his zipper. I waited in anticipation as he ran his hand along my ass again, gripping the skin, then glided his thumb closer to my hole, pressing against it. He let spit drip from his lips, the saliva dropping right on the spot.

I fought my thighs as they threatened to clench, and he landed another slap on my cheek. "Keep these legs wide open." His thumb increased pressure as he circled, wetting the area before slowly inserting the digit. I bit out a moan, a gasp escaping my lips. I'd never gone there with Chase, or any boyfriend for that matter, and I was almost thankful for Booker being the first. He was considerate of the way it might feel for me, making sure the area was wet and he slid in slowly.

With his thumb about an inch inside my ass, the head of his cock slid along my slick center. "You want me to fill you like a dirty little slut, Darlin'?"

I nodded, humming my response.

He spanked me again, the crack ringing through the barn. "Use your words like a good girl and maybe I will."

"Yes," I breathed.

I let my weight hang from the hook above me as he glided his cock inside my pussy. I bit down on my lip as his free hand grabbed my hip, keeping me steady while he pulled in and out at a tortuously slow pace. Then, his speed quickened, and he was pounding into me, my body swinging forward with each thrust.

The sounds our bodies made together as he pressed deeper into my ass with his thumb should have been vulgar, but instead, it soaked me further, and I felt drops of my arousal falling down the inside of my thighs.

With my hands tied and latched to the hook above my head, I was completely at his will for whatever he wanted to do to me. I was quickly finding it was exactly where I wanted to be—under his control. Outside of sex, I wasn't sure if I'd be okay with it. But like this? He could have his way. I fucking loved it.

"So fucking wet for me," he ground out. "You like being all tied up for me. What a dirty fucking girl."

Hums and moans rolled into one another as pressure built in my core, the length of him hitting my sweet spot just perfectly as his thumb worked my other hole. I was blissfully full of him, and the thought made me want to explode.

Gently, he pulled his thumb out. Then, in the span of a

breath, he was unhooking my arms from above, all while keeping his pace inside me from behind. A flash of metal glinted in the dim moonlight, and the bailing twine snapped as he ran a pocket knife through it seamlessly. He tossed the blade to the ground along with the string and grabbed my arms, pulling them behind my back. He eased us forward slightly, pressing my front to the stall with my cheek squished against the wood.

He fucked me like that, holding my hands behind my back so my ass was perked higher and my breasts were bouncing against the wood slats, creating friction against my peaked nipples.

"You want to come, Darlin'?"

A whimper passed my lips before I said, "Yes. Please."

He dropped one of my arms, keeping his grip tight on the other. "Rub your clit for me. I want to feel you choke my cock when you come."

I reached my hand between my legs, rubbing circles over the swollen bud. He increased his pace, thrusting into me with a speed I wasn't sure I could handle. But Booker pushed me to my limits, and my entire body was tightening.

My core clenched as my fingers quickened, then I was screaming out his name as fireworks exploded behind my eyes. Every coherent thought turned into pure pleasure as my orgasm flowed through me. Then, he was pounding deeper, harder, and exploding all the same.

I slackened against the stall as he let go of my other arm, leaving himself inside me as we caught our breath. Placing my palms against the wood, I stood straighter, feeling a slight ache in my back from where I'd hit the counter earlier, and the position I was just bent in. It was nothing compared to the heaven I just felt, not for the first time, because of Booker.

I froze as Booker's lips grazed the back of my shoulder, moving my hair out of the way to ghost his mouth over the crook of my neck. He was gone a second later, footsteps receding. "Clean yourself up and head to bed."

I spun, not giving a shit that I was naked. "Excuse me?"

He'd just fucked me like there was no tomorrow, and now he wanted to dip out?

He stopped in his tracks, facing me. He'd already situated himself back in his jeans, but he still wore his mask. "Don't fucking start, Brynne."

I grabbed my clothes from where they sat on the ground, my shirt completely ruined, and stomped toward him. "You don't get to just fuck me and then tell *me* to clean up."

He met me halfway, leaning close to my face. I wouldn't stand down—no matter how intimidating he was trying to be. "I'm not your bitch little boyfriend. You want nice and sweet? You go fuck men like Chase."

My pulse thrummed as his words hit me right where I didn't expect them to. "I want respect."

"You didn't want that while my cock was buried so deep in that tight pussy of yours, you couldn't even remember your own name."

My lips pressed into a thin, tight line. "It wasn't even that great."

He chuckled, the sound lacking any humor. "Yeah. That's why you came all over me."

Fuck, I wanted to slap him.

"You're just hiding from how you really feel," I shot out.

His teeth ground together, then he was taking his cowboy hat off and setting it on my head. I was confused for the briefest moment, until he was pulling his shirt off and shoving it at me. I took it as he retrieved his hat, my eyes fused to the tattoos and scars littering his chest and stomach. He was beautifully sculpted, like the ranch was imprinted into every divot and crevice that shadowed between bulging muscles and battle-worn skin. "Wipe yourself with it. Wear it. I don't give a shit. But that's as sweet as you're getting from me."

And for the third time, I watched Booker walk away from me without a worry in the world.

Maybe that was the way he was taught to deal with things—to just leave them behind him—but I wouldn't stand for it.

If he didn't want to admit his feelings, fine. He didn't have to. Sex didn't mean we were dating or anything. But while I lived in his house temporarily, he'd treat me like a human fucking being. I wasn't to be used as a fuck toy, no matter how appealing the thought felt at the moment. I didn't need strings, just pleasure, but already, my emotions were out for the world to see, and it was all because of Booker.

CHAPTER 11

BOOKER

"Don't mix business with pleasure. Isn't that what they say?" Austin teased from where he sat on the opposite side of the burn pile. We'd spent the day clearing some brush on the property, and as dusk fell, the debris kept on burning. About twenty minutes ago, we'd added some larger branches. Once those fizzled out, we'd head inside, but for now, we stuck around. Last thing I needed was a fire getting out of control and spreading to the land.

The amber glow from the flickering flames illuminated the space around us. We were pretty close to the driveway, the light from the barn glowing in the distance. Henley had brought some chairs out, which was where we sat now, spread out around the fire, enjoying some beers.

Without saying a word, they'd figured out the line I'd crossed with Brynne. I wasn't one to mess around with women, but something about that girl made me break the boundaries I'd set for myself. I almost wanted to hate her for it, but it was no one's fault but my own. She was in a vulnerable state right now, giving me too much power when it came to her body. If I had half a mind, I'd tell her to go find a new fuck buddy—not that that was what we were, but if she wanted orgasms, she needed to look elsewhere—but the thought of her with someone without me there, those moans of pleasure being brought on from some other asshole, made my fists twitch with the urge to beat a man black and blue.

She was here for one reason, and one reason only: to help us get the deed to the ranch back in our possession. Not to get me off. Yet, it was a plus, and I didn't want it to stop now that I knew what she felt like when she exploded around my cock, her inner walls milking every last fucking drop from me. I hadn't even thought to ask if she was clean. Fuck, at the moment, I didn't think it would have mattered. That woman was equivalent to a drug, so willing to get on her knees for me. I'd only done that to try to teach her some control with her fear, and she was bending it in all the wrong ways.

"Maybe you should tell Henley that." I mean, shit, he was the one who'd lost our fucking livelihood in a childish game of pool.

Henley threw his hands out. "Don't bring me into this. You're the one fucking her."

My eyes darkened in his direction. "I wouldn't be fucking her if you hadn't lost the deed to the only home we have." It was a poor excuse to pin the blame on him. Before finding our place on this ranch, we'd been floaters, moving from place to place until we'd conjured up enough money to purchase the land. We lived in tents for years after that, right under the old sycamore tree by the barn, as we saved up to build the house.

"You're blaming me for your dick banging the shit out of her?"

I slightly shook my head at the idiotic way he phrased it. Henley was a fucking dumbass sometimes. "I'm blaming you for her being here in the first place."

"Is it so bad if you're getting a few quick fucks out of it?" he asked.

My teeth ground together as Austin took a casual sip of his beer.

"You jealous, Hen?" Austin asked.

Henley's eyes darted to him, the flame reflecting in them as he scoffed. "I wouldn't want to fuck her with a ten-foot pole."

The insult made me want to ring his neck out, but tires crunching over gravel pulled our attention away, presumably saving Henley's life.

"Speak of the devil," Austin muttered as Brynne's car came into view.

She stopped it right outside the house, killing the headlights before turning off the car. As her form appeared in the moonlight, I found she was heading in our direction instead of into the house.

Rather than going through the gate, she hopped the fence, striding over to us in her little diner outfit. Speaking of killing someone, the length of that skirt made me want to gouge her boss's eyes out. He knew what he was doing when he made them a requirement.

"Evening, boys," she announced, not glancing my way.

My head moved as I tracked her, right to where she plopped her ass on Austin's knee.

He sat there, frozen like a statue, as Henley's brows rose.

"Good day?" she asked, like being perched on his leg was as casual as brushing her goddamn teeth.

My jaw ached as I tried to sit back in my chair, attempting to look relaxed but feeling anything but.

"It was great," Austin said, keeping his hands off her, probably assuming I'd cut them off if given the chance. Smart guy.

Internally, I chastised myself. I didn't have some fucking claim on her.

"Pretty boring if you ask me," Henley replied.

I lifted my chin in her direction. "By that little smirk on your face, looks like you had a good day yourself."

Her hand rested on her bare thigh, her position making that tiny skirt ride higher. She shrugged. "It was alright."

"Any more visitors at work?" I swigged my beer, wishing like hell the liquid would cool the fuse threatening to spark in my gut. She wasn't mine. She could do whatever the fuck she wanted.

"Nope." She popped the *P*, exaggerating the roundness of her lips as she said the word.

She was trying to get under my skin, but two could play at that game.

"Austin."

He looked in my direction.

"Put your hand between her legs, would you?"

Her lips rolled together as she stared at me. I arched a brow, silently saying *game on*.

Austin looked up at her, gauging how she might feel about that.

"Are you okay if I—"

"I didn't say fucking talk to her. I told you to move your fucking hand, so move it."

He glanced at me, unsure what my motive was here, but fuck. I didn't know, either.

His palm met her smooth skin, and the second they made contact, my jaw was clenching tighter. Slowly, he glided it between her legs, his fingers disappearing up under her skirt. The moment his hand disappeared, the fabric rose higher, revealing she wasn't wearing underwear.

Fuck me.

I nearly wanted to groan, but instead, I kept my back to the chair like this didn't bother me one bit. Brynne, keeping those beady eyes on me, looped an arm around the back of Austin's neck.

"How wet is she?" I asked, my voice an octave lower.

"Like she's been thinking about you all day."

Brynne didn't move, and from here, I could tell he swiped a finger up the center of her pussy.

"She can think about you now," I said to him, silently giving him permission to do whatever the fuck he wanted with her. *She wasn't mine.* I had to keep reminding myself of that when it should've already been ingrained in me.

She arched a brow in response, quietly sassing me.

I cocked my head to the side slightly. "Is that attitude, Brynne?"

She shrugged, pressing her breasts closer together with the move. "However you want to take it, Booker."

The use of my name sent heat straight to my cock, which was exactly what she wanted to happen.

"Austin, bend her over your knee."

She gave no reaction as his hand paused between her legs.

"Uh, Booker—"

"I didn't fucking stutter, did I?"

Setting his hands on her waist, he helped her off his knee, then guided her torso down until her stomach and chest rested across his lap. The sight of her like that made my jeans feel too damn tight.

I tipped the neck of my bottle in their direction. "Draw that little skirt of hers up."

His fingers wrapped around the hem, barely having to move it up at all for her perfect ass to be exposed. My eyes trailed down her body as he draped the skirt over her lower back.

A few feet to my right, Henley cleared his throat, adjusting in his seat. I could see the desire glowing in his eyes. *Wouldn't want to fuck her*, my ass. I'd show him exactly what he was fucking missing. Make him wish he could do the things I did to her.

"Show her what happens when she cops a fucking attitude."

Austin raised his hand, then brought it down on her cheek, the crack echoing through the dark fields around us. Brynne kept her gaze directly in front of her, holding back her reaction to the sting. I studied how she raised her ass just the slightest bit higher, begging for more.

"I don't think that did the job, Austin. What about you?"

He shook his head, dropping any hesitation he'd shown before. "Nah, I don't think so."

He glanced at me, and I dipped my chin in response.

Austin landed another slap to her opposite cheek, harder this time, and she jumped slightly, pressing her lips together.

"How wet is she now?"

He reached between her legs, dragging a finger up her center. "Soaked. She fucking likes it."

Satisfaction rolled through me, making my cock twitch.

"Why don't you feel inside her? Might be more."

He moved, sliding a finger into her drenched pussy, and I knew he'd hooked his finger deep inside her with the way her breath hitched.

"She really is a bad little slut," he said, and for some reason, I was fucking enjoying this.

I stood, setting my beer in the dirt beside my chair. "Keep that finger in her." I walked over to them, standing directly in front of her face. She looked up at me, eyes gleaming in the fire light. I crouched so we were eye level, watching her try to hide her reactions as Austin fingered her.

"You like how he feels inside you, Darlin'?"

She gave the slightest nod, a small whimper escaping her. As soon as she made the noise, Austin spanked her, making her jump again.

I straightened, unzipping my jeans and popping the button. "You want your holes filled again, don't you, little slut?"

Austin added another finger, pumping in and out of her as she tried to nod.

I pulled the top of my jeans down, freeing my cock from my restricting pants. I wrapped a fist around the base, stroking it slowly. "Wet those lips."

Her tongue darted out, coating them in saliva.

I ran the head of my cock along her mouth, then her tongue lapped at the tip, laving up the bead of moisture.

"Spit on it," I commanded.

Her lips pursed together before she did as I said, spitting on my cock. Some of it dripped off the side of my length before I pumped a fist along it.

"Open."

Those plump lips of hers parted, and I slid my cock in, her warm tongue wrapping the underside of it blissfully. All the while, Henley watched from across the fire. I was surprised he didn't try to relieve himself or leave. Instead, he just sat there, his intense gaze glued to us.

I wrapped a fist in her hair, holding her head steady as I began to fuck her mouth, gliding in and out of her as Austin continued to finger her.

"Why don't you play with her ass while you're at it, Austin," I said, burying myself deep in her mouth. Her tongue flexed as I hit the back of her throat, her eyes watering.

She moaned around me as Austin wet a third finger, sliding it into her tight little ass. I knew exactly how his finger felt in her, which only made me wrap my hand tighter in her hair. I pulled out of her mouth, drool sliding down her chin as I forced her to look up at me. Pure pleasure shone in her gaze, which was exactly what I wanted.

I glanced at Austin, and he took the signal, spanking her again. She moaned right as I forced her head back down, her lips instantly wrapping around my cock as I fucked her mouth relentlessly.

I'd never even dreamed of sharing a woman with my best friend, but the way I enjoyed Brynne being full of the two of us made me fucking feral.

Keeping her head steady, I slid down her throat, eliciting a gag. My other hand moved, plugging her nose as I stayed seated in her mouth, her tongue twitching so fucking hard against my length. I nearly fucking exploded as her throat tightened, and then I pulled out, letting her breathe.

She panted, saliva falling to the dirt at my boots, as Austin gripped her ass.

"You want to come with my cock in your mouth, Darlin'?"

She swallowed, nodding. "Yes, please."

Her plea made my cock throb.

"So needy, little slut." I slid my cock back past her swollen lips again as Austin pumped her harder, faster. Her drenched center was perfectly audible as he continued, his palm meeting the pink skin of her ass again with a crack.

I fucked her mouth just as hard, her saliva soaking her chin and neck while I did all the work.

Austin picked up speed, gripping her cheek so hard, his fingers dug into her skin. Then, her toes were lifting her ass higher, and she was moaning around my cock. As she came, I hit the back of her throat again, spilling myself inside her mouth.

There was nothing to compare to how good it felt. My release sliding down her throat as she orgasmed around Austin's fingers, her perfect, cherry red ass perked high in the air as he kept pumping her.

Finally, her body relaxed the slightest bit, and he slowed his pace, sliding his fingers out of her carefully. I pulled my cock out of her mouth, situating myself back in my pants as she breathed rapidly, trying to get herself under control.

The fire crackled beside us, the flame dying out as we all came down from whatever high overtook us. She went to push herself off his lap, and my gaze shot to Austin's hands helping her. Out of everything, that made me fucking jealous. Not him fingering her, not him wringing an orgasm out of her, but him *helping* her.

I moved without thinking, scooping her up into my arms. She let out a little shriek as I cradled her, pulling her to my chest. I didn't give a damn that her skirt dangled freely, exposing her sensitive ass. We'd all just seen her fucking come.

Without a word, I stomped away from the burn pile toward the house. With one hand, I unlatched the gate, then closed it behind us.

I had no fucking idea what I was doing, but whatever it was, I was doing it.

CHAPTER 12

BRYNNE

I didn't ask questions as Booker carried me up the steps to the porch, then shoved his way inside the house. My body was still reeling from the orgasm they'd rung from me, and I was silently thankful for not having to walk on my own. I hadn't meant for my sitting on Austin's lap to turn into what it did. I'd only meant to make Booker a little jealous. Make him regret walking away from me all those times. From the way he held me now, it seemed to do the job, but not in the way I intended.

I wouldn't complain about the two of them having their way with me, though. I'd never experienced an orgasm so powerful. But I was quickly coming to find that Booker made my body feel things it never had before. I wasn't sure if the intensity of my orgasm came from the two of them or just Booker alone. He'd looked so...possessive. Like he wanted to lay claim to me.

And I wanted to let him.

He carried me up the wide staircase, but instead of

turning down the hall in the direction of my room, he went the opposite way.

"Where are you taking me?"

His grip on me softened the slightest bit, like he didn't want me scared of what he was doing. After the experience by the fire, I was glad for it. My body was exhausted.

He brought us into a massive room, a king-sized bed directly in the center with posts on all four sides. Rather than respond, he laid me on the comforter, then crossed the open space to the attached bathroom, disappearing inside.

The sound of spraying water filled the silence, and I sat up, staring at the open doorway. He walked by the opening twice, once carrying a towel, and the second time two bottles. Then, he reappeared, crossing to the dresser.

He rifled through it like it was his own, and then it hit me. I was in his room.

Finding whatever he was looking for, he tossed two articles of clothing on the bed, then faced me. "Shower's warming up. There's a towel, some shampoo and conditioner, and body wash is in the shower. You can wear these when you're done."

I eyed the clothes. They looked to be a black shirt and gray sweatpants.

"I have clothes in my room."

He simply stared at me. "And I'm telling you you'll wear these when you're cleaned up."

He headed toward the door we'd come through.

"Wait."

He paused with a hand on the knob, looking over at where I still sat on the bed.

"Where are you going?"

"Got a ranch to take care of, Darlin'."

The words unspoken rang loud and clear. He'd paused that just to bring me in here. He could have easily let me walk inside on my own, shower in the hall bathroom, and take care of myself. But instead, he'd left his duties on the ranch for five minutes just for me—and I assumed he did it to show that he cared.

"Am I supposed to sleep in here?" I asked hesitantly.

"You can sleep wherever you want."

But there was a reason he'd plopped me on his bed and not my own.

There was also a question behind his eyes, laced with worry. Like he thought I might choose Austin's bed instead.

Without another word, he left, closing the door behind him.

I stayed on the bed another moment, letting the water have its time to warm up. The Booker I just witnessed was a night and day difference to the Booker I'd first met, and it'd only been a few days since our first interaction.

I'd thought I was a fool for allowing a man I'd just met to fuck me, and each time he walked away, I wanted to believe it was a mistake. That I wouldn't do it again. And honestly, if he had done the same today, it was likely that I *would* have walked away. But the side of this man that just presented himself to me in a quietly caring way was the treatment I wanted after all the rough sex and manhandling.

I hated admitting that I liked both parts of him, however opposite they may be, but it was what I craved.

My only fear was that the pieces of Booker I'd met so far fit the idea of a dream man in my mind almost to a T.

———

"Halloween is, like, two weeks away," McKenna said as she fixed her high ponytail.

I'd fallen asleep in Booker's bed last night, and at some point while I slept, he'd crawled in beside me, pulling me onto his chest. He was gone by the time I woke, though, and when I left for work, the three of them were out of sight, presumably doing chores out on the ranch.

"Are you dressing up?" she asked, snapping me out of the phantom memory of his body pressed to mine.

I turned to her. "Dressing up for what?"

"Halloween," she repeated. "Aren't we going to the haunted house?"

Every year, for the week leading up to the holiday, they opened the doors to the infamous haunted house that sat at the top of the hill right outside of Whiskey Ridge. And every year since we were twelve, McKenna and I would go together on opening night.

"Yeah. Of course we are."

As was the weather's usual state in October, light raindrops fell from the gray sky, landing in puddles on the sidewalks outside. My shift had gone by slow, the chilly northern Idaho weather keeping people at home rather than enjoying an evening at the diner. I wouldn't argue, though. It let my mind wander back to last night.

"Do you want to coordinate outfits?" she asked, readjusting the stack of menus that sat on the bar.

I grabbed the container of salt from under the counter, uncapping one of the shakers to refill it. "Aren't we a little old for dressing up?"

She gasped, holding a hand to her chest. "We are never too old for dressing up."

I shot her a frown, side-eying her as the salt reached the brim. Setting the jug on the counter, I screwed the cap on the glass shaker.

"Maybe sexy cheerleaders," she thought aloud, tapping a pink-painted nail to her bottom lip. It matched her lip gloss and blush scrunchie.

I gestured to our uniforms. "We already practically dress up as that every day."

She scrunched her nose. "You're right. Scratch that. How about Barbie?"

I snorted. She was the spitting image of the infamous doll. I, on the other hand, could never pass as the flawless image. "Yeah, that'd be perfect. For you."

"So grouchy today." She picked up her pen, twirling it in her fingers. "Little sleep?"

I placed the large jug of salt back under the counter, ignoring her question. "I'll come up with something."

"Oh!" she squealed, slapping her pen on the bar. "How about a cowgirl?"

"Are you just saying that because I'm living on a ranch for the time being?"

She tried to hide her smile, but failed. "No."

"Mhm." I wasn't buying it.

"It'd be perfect, Brynne!" She grabbed my arm, bouncing the slightest bit on the heel of her foot. "Booker could be your cowboy date."

I turned away, heading into the kitchen to clock out. "He's not my date."

"You'd be a sexy cowgirl, with short shorts and a hat!" She kept going, following me to the back. "I can see it now. Booker would love it."

"Booker isn't going." I wasn't even planning on asking him. He seemed like he had better things to do than hang out in some gimmicky haunted house, screaming at jump scares and being chased by actors with chainsaws.

"That's lame." She wrote her clock-out time on the paper, popping her gum as she passed it to me. I'd grown used to the sound after so many years of her chewing it. It helped with her anxiety, giving her something to do.

Once I scribbled down my own time, we headed back out to the front to close up the diner.

"I'll get our costumes together. You don't need to worry about it one bit," she said as I twisted the key in the lock.

"If anything, I should worry more."

She flipped her ponytail over her shoulder, rolling her eyes. "I have much more fashion sense than you, Brynne. You should be thanking me."

Growing up, she was the girly girl and I was the tomboy. Our friendship was definitely an *opposites attract* situation. I'd sprayed my mud pie on her new sundress, and we'd bonded over cleaning it off with the water spigot at school. The rest was history.

We walked side by side toward our cars, our sneakers sloshing in the small puddles.

"Are you heading to the ranch?" she asked, digging around for her keys in her purse as we approached the vehicles.

"I think I'm going to work out for half an hour, then make my way over there." It wasn't that I was avoiding seeing Booker, but I wasn't quite sure where I stood with the three of them, and I didn't want to just outright ask what this meant.

We were having fun. It was as simple as that.

But if that was the case, why was my mind having such a hard time wrapping around the fact that this thing with Booker was temporary?

"Alright. Well, be safe. I'll see you in a couple days."

I didn't work until the morning after the opening night of the haunted house, which was three days away. That meant I wouldn't see her until that evening.

I pulled on the handle of my car. "I trust you not to make me look like an idiot in that costume."

She opened her own door, looking over at me. "Have I ever let you down?"

The response wasn't comforting in the least. Most likely, she'd show up with lingerie and a cowgirl hat and tell me it was trendy.

"Goodnight," I called to her.

"Night!" We got in our vehicles, and I headed toward the gym as she turned the opposite way.

The local workout spot was nothing special. I liked to avoid it if I could, but now that I didn't have Chase's equipment to use, I needed a way to get some kind of a sweat going that didn't just involve running. I never did anything extreme—just the bare minimum when time allowed. Enough to make my limbs ache the slightest the next day, giving me that sense of satisfaction after a few exercises.

Parallel parking my car outside the gym, I surveyed my

surroundings before turning it off. It was no secret I was on Chase's radar, and the last thing I needed was an incident like what happened at the diner to occur out here. After grabbing the leggings and crop top I kept in my car in case of emergency from my back seat, I got out and locked the car.

Once I was inside, I changed in the locker rooms, stashing my discarded clothes in a cubby and throwing my hair in a ponytail, then got to my routine. There was only one other person occupying the space—an old man on one of the stationary bikes.

I started with a few stretches, then grabbed a ten-pound weight to do some squats and other various exercises. After thirty minutes of light weights, the burn in my thighs and butt forced me to stop. I set the dumbbell back in its spot, then hopped on the treadmill.

The old man on the bike slowed his pace, grabbing his small towel to wipe the sweat from his forehead, and got off. He didn't glance my way as he left the gym, and then I was alone.

With no one else in the vicinity, I turned on some music from my phone's speaker since I didn't have headphones with me, keeping an eye on the front door in case someone walked in. There were windows lining the street-facing side of the building, but with the mist clinging to the air, I couldn't see much through them.

I kept a steady pace as I jogged, then slowed to a walk after twenty minutes. With the memory of last night running on repeat in my mind, I should have sprinted to try to distract myself, but a big part of me wanted to keep remembering the way I'd felt with Austin and Booker both having their way with me. I didn't feel shameful of it either, not even with the knowledge that Henley watched the whole thing. I had to believe Booker did that on purpose— as a way of punishing him for losing the deed.

Once the timer hit thirty, I stopped the machine, getting off to clean up in the locker room. I splashed cold water on my face, cooling my heated skin, then grabbed a clean hand towel from beside the sink to dry myself off. I dabbed at my eyes with the soft cotton, then turned to toss it in the small hamper by the counter, but as soon as I did, I froze with my gaze locked onto the unfamiliar man that stood five feet from me in the doorway, blocking my only exit.

As if we both weighed our options, we stared at each other for a second or two. With the look on his face, it was obvious he wasn't here for a simple workout after a long day. He was here for a job, and I got the feeling that involved me. Without thinking, I threw the towel at him, darting to the left. I should've known the distraction was pointless as he tossed it to the side and caught me around the waist, lifting me off my feet.

"Let me go!" I shouted, slamming my hands on his hard back after he tossed me over his shoulder like I was as weightless as the towel. He was a beast of a man, about as bulky as Booker. I had no chance against him.

"Your little boyfriend still hasn't paid." He pulled me back over, slamming me up against the floor-to-ceiling mirror. Glass cracked behind me, and my head pulsed where it made contact with the mirror. The man wrapped a hand around my ponytail, tugging so that my neck was exposed, my head at an awkward angle. "I don't think my coworker made it clear what happens when we don't get our money."

"I don't know where he is," I gritted out at the same time a clang echoed through the room. It sounded a lot like a pocket knife being popped open.

"I don't believe you." He tugged my hair harder, and I swore a shard of glass was digging into my scalp as something wet and warm trickled down my hairline.

I tried to keep my breathing calm as my eyes landed on the knife in his other hand, but it was nearly impossible. "I broke up with him the night he won it. I haven't seen him since," I said hurriedly. The man didn't need to know about Chase coming to the diner the day after.

The cold tip of the blade met the skin on my neck, and I acted without thinking, kicking out, right between his legs. The guy let out a grunt, but he barely flinched otherwise before lashing out, slapping me straight across my face.

My cheek stung as he yanked my head forward, pressing it directly into his chest. Blindly reaching for anything to grab onto, for any way to hurt him, I found his chin and shoved, but at the angle I was in, I couldn't get enough force behind me for it to do anything but only make him angrier. His hand tightened in my hair and a scream ripped past my lips as I was pushed back up against the wall.

Lights flashed behind my eyes as my ears rang, my body fighting to stay up as tremors wracked my limbs. The realization that I was at a disadvantage here, with no weapon and barely any strength, slammed into me like a freight train.

I was going to die.

CHAPTER 13

BOOKER

Brynne was supposed to be off work forty-five minutes ago and pulling up to the ranch half an hour ago, but yet, her car was nowhere to be seen. My laptop sat on the desk in front of me, the screen the same as it was when my eyes drifted to the driveway out the window a while ago, waiting for her arrival.

Another minute ticked by, and before I could stop myself, I was shoving out of my chair, leaving the computer open. I grabbed my black cowboy hat from the hook, shoving it on my head as I passed through the kitchen.

"Where are you off to in such a rush?" Austin called over the back of the couch. Henley wasn't around, most likely off getting into more trouble, despite our advice to quit getting involved in that shit.

"Going to town." If I said it was to look for Brynne, he'd know my feelings ran too deep for her.

He turned back to the TV, an arm draped over the back cushion. "Let me know how Brynne is."

I grunted, walking out of the house to my truck. I

wasted no time, the engine roaring to life as I buckled, then headed toward town. I passed by the diner first, but moved on once I saw the restaurant was closed with the parking lot empty.

My truck slowly cruised by every side lot, not finding her vehicle. What if she was at McKenna's house, having some girl time? I was probably just overreacting when I had no business to. Turning down another block, my eyes landed on her sedan parked out front of the gym. The growing tightness in my chest eased a fraction as I realized she had only stopped for a workout after her shift. Now that I knew she was fine, I should've gone home, but instead, I pulled into the spot behind her car. A word with her definitely could have waited until she was back at the house, but I wanted it to be clear that she'd text if she was going to be late again.

Killing the engine, I got out, making my way around the front of the truck to head inside the building. The windows were foggy from the condensation outside, and there was old graffiti littering the brick. Right as I grabbed the door handle, a scream ripped through the air, and I was moving.

I crossed the gym in less than a second, following the panicked sound to the locker room. As soon as I stormed into the space and saw Brynne pinned by some man, my fists clenched so hard, my fingers nearly broke. I didn't hesitate, rushing over to them and grabbing the man's shoulder. With enough space to not accidentally hit Brynne, my fist swung, slamming into his nose. A satisfying crunch echoed as he let her go, but I didn't spare her a glance as I shoved him back, landing punch after punch into his sick fucking face.

He touched her, and that was a fucking mistake.

Brynne's rushed breaths came from behind me as the man's back hit the white cinder block wall. Blood sprayed from his mouth, nose, and other abrasions my fists brought forth. I wasn't leaving until he was fucking dead.

He tried to fight back, but he had no leverage. He wouldn't fucking get any. After a dozen or so punches, he started to slump, but I grabbed his arm, slamming it against the wall. With his palm exposed, I whipped the switchblade out of my jeans, sending the blade straight through the center of his hand. He screamed out in pain, his eyes both swollen. His face was already a deep galaxy of purples and reds.

With the knife sticking out of his palm, I grabbed his chin with my free hand, pushing his head back against the wall. "You touched the wrong fucking girl."

"Her boyfriend owes us," he croaked.

The term made my hand move on its own accord, squeezing around his fingers so they'd close over the knife in his skin. He yelled as the sharp edge ground against the tendons.

"If I let you walk away from this alive, you'll tell your boss to leave her the fuck alone." My voice boomed through the space, leaving no room for argument. "But unfortunately for you, I'm not feeling very generous tonight."

I ripped the blade from his hand, then sank it into the skin of his neck. Red splattered the wall, blood spurting to the ground as I let the man fall at my feet. I watched as he bled out, choking on the liquid. If I'd had the time, I'd have made him suffer longer. Pulled more information from him. But Brynne was behind me, potentially hurt, and for some fucking reason, I wanted to go to her more than I wanted to torture him.

As he struggled on the hard floor, I finally turned to Brynne. She was curled up in a ball, her breathing so fast, I was sure she'd pass out if she didn't calm down. I crossed to her, kneeling in front of her. Her eyes were vacant as she stared at the man on the ground.

I needed to get her out of here.

I grabbed her hands, forcing her to a stand, then wrapped one arm around her shoulder, leading her out of the locker room. Halfway across the gym, her steps faltered, and I pulled her closer to my side. "Almost there, Brynne."

As if the sound of my voice spiked her panic, her breathing came faster, and she tripped. Instantly, I scooped her into my arms, not missing a beat, and shoved out the door with my shoulder. "Few more feet."

Grabbing the handle, I opened the door to my truck and gently set her on the passenger seat. I buckled her in, then closed the door and went around to my side, sliding in beside her. As I started the truck, her breathing seemed to slow the slightest, though it wasn't much better than before.

I pulled onto the main street, speeding back toward the ranch. Austin and Henley would clean up the mess, make the body disappear, and it'd be like nothing ever happened. It wasn't the first time we'd had to hide a body.

As I turned onto the main highway that led to the ranch, Brynne's breathing picked up again, her chest rising and falling as I glanced over to find her hands shaking uncontrollably. She wouldn't make it.

Pulling into a turn-off, I kept the engine idling as I got out and went around to the passenger side. I opened the door, unbuckling her to pull her knees my way so that she was facing me. My palms, red and smeared with the man's blood, cupped her cheeks. The dim light of the cab exposed her red cheek, and it made me want to go back there and skin him alive.

"Hey. Hey," I said, softening my tone. Her eyes were frantic, tears spilling from them. My thumb stroked the soft skin of her face. "Brynne. Look at me."

She did, and I fucking hated the pain I saw in them.

"You're safe. I've got you."

Her hands came up to wrap around my forearms, her shaking limbs worrying the fuck out of me. The feeling was foreign. Why the fuck did I care so much if she hyperventilated and passed out? It'd get her to calm down. I mentally cursed myself for even thinking that. That's not what I wanted.

"Deep breaths, okay?" She tried, and I talked her through it. "Swallow your fear, Darlin'. Don't let it control you. Bend that fear to your advantage and use it as fuel."

Because if she didn't, she'd never make it through this life.

She tried to swallow, tried to nod, as she inhaled through her nose.

"That's a good girl," I murmured. I inhaled slowly, then released it through my mouth to show her, but I didn't know what the fuck I was doing. I'd never talked someone off a ledge before.

Once her chest was rising and falling at a slower rate, I noticed a portion of her hair was caked in blood. She was bleeding.

"I'm going to get you home so I can take care of you, okay? Only ten more minutes."

She nodded, her fingers digging into my arms. I let her. I'd let her do whatever she wanted if it meant she was calm. That she was okay.

I slid my hands from her cheeks, situating her back in her seat and buckling her in. After closing her door, I got back in on my side and continued on toward the ranch. Barely ten minutes later, we were pulling up the driveway and I was turning off the truck. My boots hit the dirt, and I opened her door a moment later. She'd unbuckled, her fingers unhooking from the belt as it retracted back into place.

Sliding my hand into hers, I helped her down from the truck and closed the door behind her. Keeping it grasped in mine, I led her up the porch steps and into the house. Austin and Henley were in the kitchen cooking something, and the moment they saw Brynne's current disheveled state, they paused their movements. I gave them a warning look not to say anything, and tilted my head in the direction of the door. They knew it meant they needed to clean up the mess. Usually, I'd go with them, but right now, Brynne was my top priority. I'd send them a text with the details once I got her upstairs.

Austin nodded his understanding, then tapped Henley's elbow. Brynne and I headed up to the second story, and not for the first time, I brought her to my bedroom instead of the one she was staying in. I hated that it was my first instinct, but I wanted her close and in my space.

I led her into the attached bathroom, not releasing her as I turned on the hot water faucet for the tub. I plugged the drain, then turned to her as I gave it time to fill. Her eyes were vacant, lost in space as she stood there staring at the water. I finally dropped her hand to come around behind her. The back of her hair was matted with blood, but thankfully, it was dry now, indicating the gash had clotted. I pulled her hair loose from her ponytail before coming back around to gently grip the hem of her crop top and pull it over her head. Letting it pool on the ground, I worked on getting her out of her sports bra. Once she was topless, I knelt before her to unlace her shoes, then slipped those off along with her socks. Staying crouched, I slid her leggings down, then her underwear, and helped her step out of them. By the time I undressed myself, the water was halfway up the tub. I turned the handle to stop the water.

I grabbed her hand again, helping her step into the steaming water. After she sank in, I got in behind her, placing my legs on either side of her hips. With my back to the porcelain, I eased her to my chest, wrapping my arms around her. My intention was to get her clean, but for a few moments, I could hold her. Just for tonight.

She didn't move a muscle as she sat there, my thumb running up and down her delicate skin. She was so fragile, so breakable in this moment, and a piece of me loathed that some stranger managed to break her determined attitude in the span of a few minutes. One misstep was all it took, and she was shattered.

"You want to tell me what happened?" I murmured, continuing my strokes.

I gave her a moment to decide where to start as she took a steadying breath.

"I was finishing up at the gym when he came out of nowhere," she said, her arms tensing the slightest bit. "I tried to get away, but he slung me over his shoulder and had me against the wall in seconds."

I used every piece of restraint in my body to keep my hands from tightening on her. Just the thought of some other man handling her like that had my mind slipping to dark places I wasn't sure I'd be able to pull myself out of. Not that I wanted to. I'd already proved I'd kill for her. Hurt for her.

I was quickly finding there were no limits to how far I would go when it came to Brynne.

"The glass on the mirror cut me, I think," she said, finally moving. She lifted a hand to the back of her scalp, prodding around until she winced slightly, finding the gash.

"It's not bleeding anymore," I reassured her.

She brought her hand back under the water, red seeping through the clear tub like tendrils of smoke.

"I tried to fight back," she continued, her voice gaining some of her usual self again. Determination. Strength. And that little bit of sass I was coming to like. "But it didn't go so well. And then you came in."

"Was it the same man from the diner?"

She shook her head, leaning back into me further. "No."

Knowing Chase's boss was sending multiple people to threaten her for answers didn't comfort me in the slightest.

They wanted what he had, and they were determined to get it by whatever means necessary.

Unfortunately for them, I didn't allow anyone to put their hands on what was mine, and until I got that deed back, Brynne was mine to protect. I wouldn't let them use her as some chess piece because of her ex-boyfriend.

Silently, I wet her hair in the tub, not caring about the red tinge the water turned as I did. I washed her hair, scrubbed every inch of her body with soap, then helped dry her off afterward. Once she was in bed, wrapped in my shirt, I went downstairs to wait for Austin and Henley to get home.

I had a plan.

Chapter 14

Brynne

B ooker had left two pills and a glass of water on the bedside table, and I was thankful for it when I woke up at the crack of dawn the morning after the attack. My head pounded, but about an hour after taking the medication, I was feeling good enough to get out of his bed.

I'd slept so hard, I wasn't sure if he'd joined me at all during the night. There was a mess at the gym, and I assumed Austin and Henley would take care of the deceased man for him, but I wouldn't have doubted it if he helped in some way. Hiding a body didn't seem like an easy task, and I was sure the last place any of them wanted to end up was prison for murder.

I fixed my hair in the mirror above his dresser, then headed downstairs. As soon as I reached the last step, I found the three of them staring at me from the living room. Austin was bent over his knees on the couch, hands clasped between his legs, as he studied me. Henley was in the chair by the bookcase, and Booker was sitting on the edge of the loveseat.

"Good morning?" The greeting sounded more like a question as it seemed almost like they were waiting for me.

Booker's eyes trailed my body, likely checking for any injuries that may have gone unaccounted for last night. He knew there were none, though. He'd dried every inch of my skin so gently, looking closely for any bruising or abrasions.

"We have a plan," Austin said, straightening so his back hit the couch.

Booker nudged his chin in the direction of the cushion beside him, and I crossed to it, propping myself on the edge of the seat as I looked at them all expectantly.

Henley had this guilty look on his face, like he thought this was his fault. While in the beginning, it may have been, it was clear the rest of this was Chase's doing. Him not handing over the deed to his boss was the problem, not necessarily anything Henley did.

"You're going to text Chase to meet you somewhere," Henley said, taking the reins.

"Why would I do that?"

This time, Austin spoke up. "So we can get the deed back."

"And then what?"

"We'll kill him," Booker stated beside me.

My eyes darted to him. "Kill him?"

"We can let him go," Austin suggested, almost like he was repeating the idea for a second time.

"No. I want him dead." Booker's voice left no room for argument.

"Why?" I asked.

"Because he's proved to be a problem." But he didn't say who he became a problem for. I knew he didn't want him dead just for his own benefit. Something in him had changed, and I had the biggest feeling it had to do with me being a target.

"What if he doesn't have the deed?" For all we knew, he gave it to someone else entirely, or the bank.

Austin held his hands out, palms up, like the answer was obvious. "Then we'll get him to tell us where it is."

"You make it sound so easy," I said. Chase was stubborn, and getting him to talk wouldn't be a piece of cake, especially when the subject had to do with his earnings.

"A little pain goes a long way." At Booker's words, I looked over at him.

What he didn't say was that seeing me in the state I was in last night fueled this, and he wanted to get things moving. I wasn't going to be the one to tell these guys what to do. If they wanted to torture him, then so be it.

Anything to get this over with sooner was better in my book.

———

Booker hadn't expected me to do any chores today, but staying in bed resting seemed like a boring way to pass the time, so I'd tidied up the barn, sweeping hay and dirt from the aisles while they worked out on the ranch.

We'd eaten dinner together at the large dining table inside, and afterward, we'd all retired to our respective rooms. I was antsy for what was to come, so after a few minutes in bed, I'd pulled on my running shoes and headed outside for some fresh air.

The silence of the ranch was comforting with a mind so loud. All day, my thoughts strayed to last night, and now, with the crickets chirping under the nearly-black sky, my head was quiet. A welcome reprieve.

I walked along the fence to the pasture, my sneakers crunching over the loose pebbles in the dirt. I watched as plumes of loose dust kicked up around my ankles, and when I looked forward, I stopped in place.

There was someone on the road.

Narrowing my eyes, I saw the outline of a horse with its rider, the silhouette of a cowboy hat lit by the fading sky. We stared at each other, the both of us not making a move. My heart thumped in my chest, despite knowing it had to be Booker. He must have heard me leave the house and followed after me.

Without any warning, the horse took off at a gallop toward me, and I turned, running the opposite direction back to the barn. Hooves clomped furiously over the ground as I sprinted, but my pace was no match to the animal. In seconds, a rope was slung over me, clasping my arms to my sides. I slowed, the horse sprinting past me as its rider jumped to the ground. Large, familiar arms came around me, lifting me off the ground. I shrieked in between rapid breaths.

"I can feel your heart, Darlin'." His fingers gripped the back of my thigh where I lay over his shoulder, the lasso still tight around my upper body. "Are you scared?"

"No." Adrenaline rushed over me, but it wasn't fear I

felt. It was anticipation of what was to come. There had to be a reason he was doing this.

"That's too bad." We headed into the barn, and he tossed me on the stack of bales, the hay poking my bare legs. I instantly regretted wearing shorts between the cold and the itch. He pulled the lasso up over my body, tossing it to the ground behind him.

I looked up at him to find he was wearing the same skeleton mask he had before, his cowboy hat pulled low over his brow. He braced both hands on either side of me, leaning into my space so that I had to press my back against the bale behind me. "I want you scared when I fuck this tight little pussy." His hand was between my legs in a flash, finding my entrance easily through the leg hole of my shorts. He slid a finger in, my legs instantly going slack.

My mouth parted, and he wrapped his other hand around my neck, squeezing slightly to cut off my air. The back of my head pressed against the bale as my eyes closed, his finger pumping in and out of me quickly.

"Open those eyes, Darlin'. I want to see."

I did, and satisfaction rolled over his features as he added another finger, fucking me with his hand relentlessly.

"My little slut is always so wet for me," he muttered, adding a third.

The sensation was fucking heaven.

He released my neck, letting me breathe. I sucked in air as he suddenly removed his fingers to grab something off the wall beside us. Upon closer inspection, I found he was holding a lead rope. He pulled the rope through his hand, then looped it around my neck and tied it.

"I want you to use your fear as fuel." He pulled the rope tighter, bringing me closer to him. "Deep breath, Darlin'."

I inhaled, and then he was cutting off my oxygen again, pulling the rope tight. My mouth opened, warmth pooling in between my legs as he inserted three fingers again. He hooked them deep inside me, quickening his pace as he fucked me with them.

Black spots dotted my vision right before he loosened the rope, letting me breathe. I sucked in air as he removed his fingers from my pussy, then yanked my shorts off along with my panties. He instantly grabbed my hips, flipping me over on all fours so that I was completely exposed to him.

With a glance over my shoulder, I saw him wrap the lead rope around his fist as he yanked down his zipper with his other hand. Freeing his cock, he trailed it up my pussy, soaking the tip. Right before he slid inside me, he pulled on the rope, the circle tightening around my neck and cutting off all air again.

"Fuck, Brynne," he hissed as he seated himself in me. "So fucking tight when you can't breathe."

I tried to moan, but nothing came out as my throat was constricted. He slid out, only to pound back in, sliding my knees forward slightly on the bale. As he fucked me, he loosened the rope once more, oxygen filling my starved lungs.

"Such a dirty fucking slut. You love when I use you, don't you?"

I hummed a response, and he tugged the rope in silent reprimand before landing an ear-piercing smack across my ass. "Yes. I love it."

He fucked me harder, without restraint, and then my

ability to breathe was cut off again, my neck being yanked back, forcing my head to tilt slightly. Stars flew across my vision, from pleasure or lack of oxygen, I wasn't sure, but I never wanted the sensation to stop. Booker was playing with my fear, and it only fed my impending orgasm more.

He landed another slap on my ass, one cheek and then the other, my pussy clenching around him so hard I wasn't sure how he was still able to move in and out of me.

"Just like that, little slut. Grip my cock while I choke that pretty little neck of yours."

Right when I thought I may not be able to take any more, he loosened the rope, allowing me to breathe. Booker was in complete and utter control, and I didn't want it any other way.

His palm met my ass again, the sting coursing pleasure through me. I reached between my legs, lowering my chest to the bale. The hay poked at my skin, but I ignored it as my fingers ran circles over my clit, and he spanked me again, harder this time.

"Deep breath, Brynne. You're going to need it."

As soon as I inhaled, he was pulling the rope tight again, yanking my neck back with my chest to the bale. My fingers picked up speed, his cock following suit as he fucked me harder, faster. He groaned as my core tightened, choking his cock at the same time.

He didn't let up on the rope as he continued pounding into me, and my orgasm began to ripple through me like a firework in the night sky. Somehow, the lack of being able to breathe fueled me more, and pure heaven coursed through every inch of my body.

At the same time, he buried himself deep inside me

while finally slackening the rope fully. My moans and gasps filled the barn as his free hand gripped my hip.

He filled me, and as soon as he pulled out, I felt our release dripping down my thighs.

I kept my chest to the bale, giving myself a moment to breathe, but my breath hitched as he trailed his finger up my thigh, through our mess, and shoved it back in my pussy.

He slid in and out of me a few times, my entrance and clit sensitive from my orgasm. My legs tensed as he took his fingers out.

I pushed up off the bale, turning around to face him. Unexpectedly, he tightened the rope around my neck again, forcing me to look up at him as he hovered over me with my chest pressed to his still-hard cock. My knees bit into the bale below me. "The only one you need to be afraid of in this world is me, Brynne. Anyone else, and I won't hesitate to kill them." He brought his face closer to mine. "I own that part of you."

He stared into my eyes for a moment, making sure his words set in the way he wanted them to. With his gaze glued to mine, he said, "You can come in now."

Behind him, Austin rounded the corner, entering the barn. He wore a similar mask, the skeleton only covering half his face. My body somersaulted with the thought of him having heard everything Booker and I just did, and how I still sat exposed with the rope around my neck.

"He's been waiting the whole time, Darlin'," Booker murmured to me, almost like he cared about filling me in on Austin's presence. "Are you okay with him joining?"

With a swallow, I nodded.

Booker's eyes scanned mine behind his mask, darting between the two like he was searching for the truth in my response. "You want to have your fun with her?" he asked Austin.

A playful smirk crested Austin's lips. "Took you long enough." He removed his hand from behind his back, producing my vibrator. He must've found it in my room, and the thought of him in there without me somehow made my skin heat.

Booker set a boot up on the bale, hopping up to sit on the one directly behind me so that I sat perched between his legs. He kept his hold on the lead around my neck loose enough so that it didn't choke me—for now.

"Take your spurs off," Booker commanded.

Austin did, unbuckling them from around his boots. He handed one to Booker, keeping the other for himself. Then, Austin slid my shirt over my head, and Booker slid it the rest of the way off, untangling it from the rope.

Booker pulled up on the rope, causing me to crane my neck as it tightened. As my ability to breathe became harder, Austin reached forward and pulled the cups of my bra down so my breasts spilled over the top, full and on display.

Booker slackened the rope. "Be a good little slut and stick that tongue out, Darlin'."

I did, right as Austin's knees met the ground before me. He pulled me forward so my ass hit the edge of the bale, then pried my legs apart as Booker reached around me, sticking two fingers down my throat. I gagged as he pulled them out, bringing them down to my nipple to wet the peak.

In front of me, Austin brought the spur to the inside of my thigh, the spikes prodding at my sensitive skin. At the same time, Booker pinched my nipple, tugging it slightly. I moaned as Austin glided the spur between my legs, gently coasting it over my clit. I whimpered, and Booker tightened the rope again, cutting off my breathing. No sounds came out as Austin rolled the rowel back and forth over the swollen bud. Booker wrapped his palm around my breast, squeezing.

Every nerve inside me was more alive than ever, all over every inch of my body, and I wasn't sure if I could take the overwhelmingly blissful sensations so soon after having just come.

Right as my lungs began to burn, Booker slackened the rope again. I gasped for air as Austin kept his eyes on me. I could see his boner clear as day, bulging through the fabric of his jeans, but I wasn't sure if Booker wanted me to pleasure him. He seemed to be fine with them doing things to me, but he might not feel the same the other way around.

Austin trailed the rowel over my tender entrance, and my stomach twitched as my breath hitched. Bringing it up and down once more, he dropped it to the floor, then plunged two fingers inside me. I called out, throwing my head back as Booker wrapped a calloused hand around my exposed throat to keep me arched.

Austin's fingers thrust in and out of me, the wetness from our release evident in the sounds that came from my pussy.

Booker brought his face closer to mine. "You like when we have our fun with you, don't you?"

I moaned a response. I fucking loved it.

Austin had a hand on my thigh, keeping my legs apart as his fingers continued their haste.

"Maybe our little slut will squirt for us," Austin said, picking up his pace.

Booker's thumb coasted over my pulse before letting go of my neck. He grabbed the spur where he'd set it beside him on the bale, then glided it over my nipple. The pinpricks of pain sent pleasure coursing through me, and I wanted to scream.

"What do you say, Darlin'? You gonna soak my best friend?"

Austin's fingers dug into my thigh as his pace quickened impossibly more. He released my thigh, grabbing the vibrator and clicking it on. Instantly, the humming tip was on my sensitive clit before I could reply, and electricity wrapped around my nerves as I twitched under the overwhelming sensation. Booker dropped the spur with a clang, gripping my breast punishingly. He tightened the rope again, cutting off my air. Austin went faster still, the pressure building in my lower belly as the tips of his fingers hit my sweet spot repeatedly. Right when I thought it was too much, too overwhelming for my body to take, he withdrew his hand in a flash, keeping the vibrator over my bud, and liquid spurted from me like never before.

Right as I exploded, Booker dropped the rope, and I screamed. He kept his hand on my breast, the other cupping my neck again as I let go, every ounce of my control slipping. My thighs quivered as Austin held them open with his soaked hand, and when I managed to look down, my orgasm ebbing, I found his shirt soaked and his chin dripping. He removed the toy, my body instantly relaxing the slightest bit.

My chest heaved as Booker slowly released my breast to trail his hand up my collarbone. He gripped my chin, tilting my face up to him to bring his lips to mine. He'd taken the mask off, leaving his face bare. I froze for a millisecond. Booker was kissing me for the first time, and I had no idea what to make of it. His tongue got lost in my mouth, dancing with mine as my mind whirled.

Thus far, it'd seemed like he wanted to keep it strictly physical, and kissing felt...intimate. Like we were crossing a line he wanted to keep carefully drawn.

He pulled away, not making eye contact as he slid the lead rope off my neck and over my head. He tossed it to the ground, and when I looked forward again, I found Austin had already left.

Booker stood, hopping off the bale. He helped me up, pulling my panties and shorts back up my legs. Sliding his shirt off, he situated it over my head and helped pull my arms through. Then, he scooped me up in his arms, and we were heading out of the barn and to the house.

I wasn't sure what was happening between me and Booker, but a part of me truly was scared of him. Not in that I thought he'd hurt me, but in the feelings of mine that could be broken if I got too attached. I was fresh out of a toxic relationship, and though Booker was closed off, I felt happier with our arrangement than I ever did with Chase.

And in my experience, when I attached happiness to a person, it was all too quickly taken right out from under my feet.

I only had to hope that after this was all said and done, Booker would let me down easy.

CHAPTER 15

BOOKER

I shouldn't have kissed her. I also shouldn't have brought her into my shower last night and let us wash each other with soap. But alas, I'd done both, and now I was royally regretting it. Brynne was here for one reason, and that was to get the damn deed back for this fucking ranch. Not to chisel her way into my granite heart and make me fucking feel.

I'd left her in my bed this morning—because of course, she'd slept next to me—and found Austin and Henley in the kitchen. Austin was lucky. He wasn't the one falling for a girl he had no business catching feelings for. He had his fun with her, and walked away without a worry in the world. But me? I'd started caring for her after the first time I made her come uncontrollably, and that's where I was going wrong. For some fucking reason, though, I couldn't fucking stop.

The woman had wrapped herself around my head— both of them.

"She sending the text today?" Austin asked, not looking up from where he sliced into a sausage.

I stared at the knife in his hand, hesitating, which was a mistake, because Austin's eyes shot to me. "Oh no."

I looked at him. "What?"

"Don't tell me you're feeling soft."

I shifted on my feet the slightest bit, but of course he fucking noticed that, too.

He set the knife down on the counter. "She's here for a reason, Booker."

"Well the fuck aware," I said, biting out each word.

Henley shook his head where he sat, as if he had a fucking right to be disappointed in me.

I pinned my glare on him. "You got something to say, asshole?"

He looked at me like he was fucking innocent in this. "Don't lose sight of the plan."

I scoffed, stepping closer to him so he had to tilt his head up at me. I only had a couple inches on him, but it made all the difference in the world right now with him perched on his seat. "We wouldn't need this fucking plan if you hadn't gotten us into this bullshit mess in the first place."

Henley stood, the stool tipping over onto the tile floor. "Don't take your feelings for her out on me."

One more step, and our noses were nearly touching. "Or what, Henley? Huh? It's not like you can do any more damage than you've already done."

Then, his fist swung, and my jaw snapped to the side. My nostrils flared as I tried to keep my calm, tasting blood in my mouth from where the inside of my cheek had snagged on my tooth. Austin stood to the side, shaking his head. But it wasn't him who kept me from swinging. It was the little pitter patter of feet coming down the stairs.

"Good morn— Oh my fuck! What happened?" Brynne rushed over, stepping in front of me and placing those delicate little hands on my face to turn it every which way like she was a fucking nurse or something.

I batted her hands away, stepping back. "Nothing."

Hurt flashed in her eyes, but I pretended I was blind. She was coming in between us, and I couldn't let that happen. We needed this ranch, otherwise we had nothing.

Henley stood there, remorse clear on his face. I wouldn't hold his punch against him. Even I could admit, I may have been out of line. It was simply because she was brought up, and I hated how fucking protective I got with just the thought of her. She was a disease, infecting my very blood.

"You still in?" Austin asked her from the other side of the island.

She turned to him, and that almost hurt more than her glare. I wanted those eyes back on me.

She nodded. "I'm in."

"She's out."

All eyes turned to me, but mine were so focused on her, I didn't give a shit about the other two in the room.

"You don't get to tell me what to do," Brynne said, as if I hadn't been doing that since that night in her motel.

"You could get hurt." And that wasn't something I was willing to risk. Not after finding her in the gym, feeling her shake in my arms, hearing her panicked breaths in my truck.

"Then I get hurt," she said, like that was a fucking

option. I started to protest, but she cut me off. "Anything for the ranch, right?"

My eyes narrowed in response, my jaw going stiff.

If she wanted it her way, then fine.

"You remember the plan, then, right?" I asked, my words clipped.

She nodded, and I wanted like nothing else to fuck the furrow out of her brow, to erase any concern that clouded her mind.

I realized then that Brynne couldn't be temporary. Not with the way she infiltrated the fortress I'd put around myself when it came to women. They were nothing but trouble, but something about her erased any doubts I once had, making me want to claim her again and again until the only name she knew was mine and hers, together.

———

Brynne had sent the text two hours ago for Chase to meet her at the gas station off eighty-two at nine tomorrow morning. After she'd sent it, she'd disappeared upstairs and hadn't come down since. I sat in my office for the past hour and a half, waiting for her to return. I watched the clock tick by as I stared at my blank computer screen, and with another minute wasted, I shoved out of my chair, heading for the stairs. She could be mad—hell, she could hate me—but she couldn't hide.

Peeking in my room, I found it empty, which boiled my blood the slightest bit. I hadn't demanded she move into my space, or told her that was where she'd be staying until this was over, but knowing she was in her temporary room pissed me off.

I stomped down the hall, my boots echoing off the hallway walls as they pounded on the hardwood. Without a knock, I swung her door open to find her lying in bed on her stomach, her elbows digging into her pillow by the headboard. She was on her phone, and when the door slammed into the wall, she jumped, her eyes shooting to me.

"What the fuck, Booker?" she shrieked, dropping her phone.

I stormed over to her, grabbing her by the back of her neck, and crashed my lips to hers like a fucking idiot. I wasn't thinking. Never when I was around her.

I slid my tongue past her plump lips, tangling it with hers as she threaded her fingers through my hair, unexpectedly tugging me closer. I'd half expected her to slap me, and I probably would've been fine if she did, but this was beyond what I anticipated. I didn't want her to hate me—to think I didn't want her hands on me. Fuck, I wanted every ounce of her attention.

I pulled back, sliding my hand around her neck to grip the front. Shoving her back, I pinned her to the mattress, crawling on top of her. I let her breathe—for now.

"You want to make your own decisions, Darlin'?"

She nodded, my hand slightly constricting the motion.

"Then do it. But I won't let you put yourself in danger. Not for me."

She wrapped a hand around my arm, the limb small in comparison to mine. "You'll be there. I won't get hurt."

God, I hated the way my throat tightened. How my

tongue tripped over itself. What the fuck was she doing to me?

I leaned closer to her, adding pressure to her neck. "I won't let a soul lay a hand on you unless I allow it."

Her cheeks tinged a bright pink as her eyes watered the slightest, and I wanted nothing more than to bury my cock so far in her pussy that she had that same expression on her face. I released her, and as she gasped, I flipped her over, hiking her ass up high. She was still fully clothed, so I hooked my fingers in the hem of her shorts, yanking them down around her thighs along with her underwear.

Her pussy glistened in the light as I pressed a hand to her back, lowering her chest to the mattress. "My little slut is always so fucking ready for me."

She turned her head, looking over her shoulder at me as I visually devoured the sight of her exposed like this. Without hesitation, I leaned forward, burying myself between her cheeks. I dragged my tongue down her crack to her center, reveling in the taste of her. My cock twitched behind my jeans as I speared my tongue inside her, tasting her sweetness. She moaned into the bed as she rubbed her pussy along my mouth.

I straightened, grabbing her hips to keep her steady before using one hand to free myself from my jeans. I was a rock, my cock thick and heavy with the need for her. She was the world's sweetest craving, and I had her all to myself.

Spitting a drop of saliva on my cock, I ran my hand along my length twice, wetting every inch of the skin. I aligned the head of my cock with her entrance, and she tried to rock back, but I spanked her in warning. "Such a needy slut. I should punish you for that little move."

She groaned, swaying her hips side to side like she was practically begging me to.

I smirked. The woman wanted what she wanted. I could only deliver her wishes.

My palm met her ass hard, the slap ringing through the room along with her yelp.

"I don't know if that was hard enough," she challenged, her voice slightly muffled with the blanket as she rocked her hips back again.

My cock fucking surged with her words. Bringing my hand back, I spanked her again, harder this time, and my handprint instantly painted her cheek.

"Just like that, Nightmare," she managed to get out, her voice full of breath.

Gripping her ass, I slid my cock inside her, burying myself to the hilt. Granting her wish, I spanked her again, her pussy clenching around my length with the act.

"Fuck, Brynne," I hissed. She was so fucking *naughty*.

Pulling out to the tip, I pounded back into her, shoving her forward slightly on the bed. Then, I lost control, fucking her relentlessly. I watched as my cock slid in and out of her slick pussy, her ass pressing against me every time I hit that spot deep inside her that I knew made her crazy.

My eyes landed on her vibrator sitting on the night-stand, so I reached over to grab it. I set the toy in her hand after clicking it on. "Put that on your clit and don't you dare fucking take it off until I say so."

Her hand disappeared between her legs, her body instantly tensing as it purred over her sensitive bud. Her gasp filled the room as I spanked her again, her cheek reddening further from my hand.

I gripped her hips, my fingers digging into her flesh as I went fucking feral. Her body slid up the bed further as I let go of her hip, grabbing her hair in a fist. I yanked her head back, her pretty little neck exposed as she moaned.

"You like when I fuck you like my dirty little slut, don't you? Like it when I fill this needy pussy to the brim."

"Yes, Nightmare," she breathed, clicking up the speed on her vibrator.

Her pussy began to clench, her thighs shaking as I fucked her with no restraint, and then she was screaming, her sounds filling the room. Her hand went to fall to the bed, but I grabbed her wrist, keeping the vibrator pressed firm to her clit. Her orgasm wracked through her body in waves, her pussy so tight around my cock that it ripped my own release out of me. I spilled into her, filling her tight entrance full of me.

I finally released her wrist, the toy falling to the mattress. She lay limp, so I picked it up to turn it off. Setting the vibrator to the side, I pulled out of her, watching as our release dripped from her center. Like before, I trailed my fingers through it, shoving it back deep inside her. Her belly jumped as I did, then I pulled them out and straightened her legs so she was lying on her belly on the bed.

I tugged her shorts and underwear the rest of the way down, then got off her to go into the bathroom across the hall. Letting the water warm up, I grabbed a washcloth from under the sink and soaked it, wringing out the excess water. I turned off the faucet, going back to her room to find her in the same position I'd left her in. Her breathing was deep, and I assumed she'd most likely fall asleep soon.

I kneeled behind her, wiping between her legs with the damp cloth. I cleaned her skin, then stood, pressing a kiss to her temple. Her eyes were closed, her lips parted, so I left her there to nap, closing her door with a soft *snick*.

I tossed the washcloth in my hamper, then headed downstairs to take care of a few ranch chores before we turned in for the day. All the while, I forced any lingering anxiety about tomorrow away.

I never worried about myself—not in any situation, really—but tomorrow, my senses would be on high alert.

Brynne's safety in this was my top priority, and it was the only thought that raced through my mind as the day passed by, turning to night when the sun sank below the horizon.

Tomorrow would go as planned.

I wouldn't allow it to be any other way.

CHAPTER 16

BOOKER

To my surprise, Chase had agreed to meet Brynne at the gas station. He hadn't questioned it or seemed skeptical in the least in his text response, but I tried not to look into it as we couldn't tell the tone of his voice through a screen. For all we knew, he was that bent out of shape about Brynne leaving him that he'd do anything she asked, meet her anywhere she wanted, just for a chance to beg for her back.

"You're staying in the truck," I grumbled as I pulled into the parking lot of the gas station.

"No." Her finger was tapping an unsteady rhythm on her thigh. If she wasn't wearing jeans, she'd have poked a hole clean through her flesh by now.

"It's not up for debate." We'd already had this argument at the ranch, and of course, she'd been adamant then as well.

"He's my ex."

My grip tightened on the steering wheel at the reminder. "An ex who might want you dead."

"He's not like you," she said, silently referencing the man I'd killed in the gym.

Brynne didn't know Chase might end up like him tonight if things went south. I couldn't promise I wouldn't just shoot the man in cold blood for simply having touched her in the past.

I pulled into one of the parking spots away from the pumps and shifted into park. I left the truck running, but I didn't unlock the doors.

"Henley and Austin will take care of it." They were pulling in on the other side of the lot so it didn't look suspicious that we were together. That, and I wanted eyes on all angles in case Chase tried anything. Brynne was here to point out when Chase arrived, and I was here to keep Brynne under control. We each had a job today, and Brynne getting out of this damn truck—

The passenger door opened, and my gaze darted to the sound right as Brynne slid out. I reached for her, but the woman slipped just past my grip.

Sneaky fucking girl. She unlocked the damn door herself. I shouldn't have expected anything less.

Yanking my seat belt off, I situated my mask over my face to keep myself hidden and pulled the handle so hard I thought it might snap. I rushed over to her where she was walking toward a gray sedan.

"Brynne," I hissed, quickening my pace.

The driver's side door to the car opened, and the barrel of a gun glistened in the sunlight. I darted for her just in time for the shot to ring out, tackling her to the ground and covering her with my body.

Footsteps sounded on the pavement as Austin and

Henley rushed over. Another shot rang out as I looked up, finding Austin ripping open the passenger door on the sedan. Gun in hand, Henley came around the trunk. They were both wearing their skeleton masks to hide their identities as well. While Chase was distracted with Austin invading the vehicle, Henley aimed and took the shot. Instantly, blood stained Chase's khakis, and he dropped his pistol to the asphalt with a shout. He tried to cover the wound, but it was pointless as blood flowed freely. His wrist was in a cast, presumably from when I shattered the bone.

With the weapon out of his hand, my attention snapped back to Brynne. Her hands were pressed to the ground, her cheek squished against the pavement with my body over hers. My hands frantically coasted down her body, feeling for any blood.

"Brynne, Darlin', talk to me. Tell me you're okay."

She coughed, presumably from the air being knocked out of her not moments ago. I shoved up off the ground, my eyes searching her body. Grabbing her shoulder, I flipped her onto her back, checking her torso.

"I'm okay," she croaked before coughing again. She had tiny pebbles stuck to her rosy cheek along with indentations freckling her arms from the debris.

I felt bad for crushing her, but fuck, it was better than her getting shot. Anything was.

With one last in-depth visual search of her body, I moved my gaze to the guys where they had Chase pinned to the ground, his wound oozing blood onto the pavement.

"Get the fuck off of me!" He squirmed, but Austin had his knee pinning his hands behind his back, cast and all.

Henley was picking up the gun with a towel, shoving it into a clear plastic bag.

Thankfully, the gas station was empty save for us, and whoever worked inside hadn't come looking to see what chaos had caused the gunshots. Smart thinking, because otherwise, I'd have to take care of two bodies today.

I stood, grabbing Brynne's hands to pull her up in front of me.

"Get in the truck," I instructed, guiding her behind me. Who the fuck knew if Chase had friends waiting to take care of this mess if he wasn't successful.

"I'm not just going to stand by and let you guys take care of all of this."

I spun on her, our faces merely an inch apart. "Yes, you are."

She tipped her chin up, crossing her arms over her chest. There was barely any room between the two of us to do so. "Why can't I help, Booker?"

My lips pressed into a thin line.

She knew the fuck why. She was asking simply to make me say the words.

She tilted her head slightly, aiming her ear my way. "Hmm, what was that, Nightmare? I didn't hear you."

"This isn't the time for games, Brynne."

She straightened her head, fluttering her lashes. "Then admit it, and it won't be a game."

I scoffed, subtly shaking my head. She was ridiculous. She was just shot at by her fucking ex, her life was in literal danger, and she wanted me to get fucking sappy?

Pass.

I leaned closer. "There's nothing to admit, Darlin'."

Her eyes flashed, but she covered it up seamlessly. "Admit you don't want me hurt because you care about me."

"I only care about keeping you alive until this is all done. Then you're free to do whatever the fuck you want."

I regretted saying it the moment the words left my mouth, but I needed her in the goddamn truck and out of harm's way. If being the villain was what it took to keep her safe, I'd be the fucking villain.

The lie hit its mark, and she turned on her heel, striding back to the truck without so much as a glance over her shoulder. With her posture alone, I could tell I'd hurt her. Maybe not physically, but damn well emotionally. I watched until she closed herself in on the passenger side, then I headed over to Austin and Henley to help them get Chase in the back of Henley's SUV.

By the time I made it over to them, they'd already zip-tied his wrists behind his back and were escorting his limping form to the trunk. He was spewing curse words at them left and right, taking his sweet ass time.

I came up behind him, shoving him forward so that he had no choice but to walk faster.

"What the fuck?" he hissed, nearly collapsing on his injured leg. "I'm fucking shot, dude!"

"Cry me a fucking river," I snapped.

Henley was making sure the tarp was taped down securely while Austin walked alongside Chase, ushering him to the vehicle. With a hard push, he landed chest-first on the plastic layer coating the trunk. We'd brought it as a precautionary method in case he got any hair or saliva anywhere, but now that he was bleeding, it came in handy tenfold.

Austin swung Chase's legs in, then set a hand on the trunk handle.

Chase twisted, panicked eyes darting between us. "Where are you taking me?"

I stepped back, giving Austin space to close the back.

"To your own personal hell."

———

Horses got injured all the damn time, so a little blood on the rubber mats wouldn't be suspicious. The multiple hoses and drains were convenient for later, hence why Chase was currently tied to a chair in the middle of the wash rack, his hands and legs bound to weathered wood. We hadn't been soft with his broken wrist, and we'd heard all about it the entire time we tied him up. I didn't give a fuck. He didn't deserve an ounce of mercy.

He let out a muffled shout, trying to say something through the cloth looped around his head to keep him quiet. He'd started screaming the moment the rope was tight around his wrist, so I'd finally shut him up. He could yell all he wanted—there was no one to save him out here—but my sanity needed the fucker to quit his complaints.

Brynne hadn't said a word to me on the drive back and went straight into the house after we pulled into the driveway. I'd wanted to go after her, to explain that I only said what I said to keep her safe, but I had other things I needed to take care of first. The fact that I had to choose between her and Chase only made me hate him more. I'd get the information we needed out of him, and then he'd be off my hands, and I could go make things right with the woman in our house.

I couldn't believe I was even thinking those words, but here I was.

In the aisle of the barn, the propane forge burned bright, heating up the metal on the fire poker. I would've used our branding iron, but I didn't want any ties to this ranch with what we were about to do.

Henley set the fifth bucket of water by the wall, wiping his hands on his jeans. The autumn night air held a chill, a coyote howling somewhere in the distance, as I nodded at Austin. He stepped toward Chase, whose eyes were frantic as they darted around, looking every which way. Austin pulled the cloth down to his neck, then retreated a few feet, crossing his arms.

Chase sucked in quick breaths, his chest heaving against the ropes. "What do you want from me?"

I held his gun in my gloved hand, holding it up to admire it like I'd never seen such a weapon before, but in reality, I was all too familiar with how to handle the firearm. "Not going to ask where your girlfriend is?" I fucking *hated* putting the claim on her like that, but I wanted him riled up.

His brows pulled inward for a split second, enough time to indicate he'd completely forgotten she was a part of this. What a fucking dick.

Chase pointed his eyes at me. "Where is she?"

I dropped the gun to my side, my finger off the trigger with the barrel pointed at the ground. "In my bed."

The vein in Chase's neck bulged as realization hit him. In his mind, she was fucking the wrong side.

"Why'd you shoot at her?" I asked, casually starting to circle him where he sat.

"I was aiming at you," he bit out.

We both knew that was a lie.

I came around his side, bringing the tip of the barrel to his chin to tilt it upwards. "Why'd you try to shoot Brynne?"

This wasn't the objective here. All we needed was to figure out where the deed to the ranch was, and we could kill him. Yet here I fucking stood, playing protector over a woman who wasn't even mine.

"I told you, I wasn't trying to hit her."

I cocked the hammer back with my thumb. A bead of sweat rolled down Chase's temple to his jaw, dripping onto the mat without a sound, along with the rest of his perspiration and other various bodily fluids that would be washed away later, along with his soul.

"This time, I only want the truth."

His neck bobbed as he swallowed, choking out a breath. "Okay. Okay! She's the only one who knows where I might go to hide. If she's dead, she can't tell anyone."

I hesitated a moment, letting him wonder if I believed it or not, then lowered the gun, stepping away from him. "Why do you need to hide?"

He was setting this up perfectly to spill about the deed. It was almost too easy.

"I already told you why I shot at her. That's why I'm here, isn't it? So you can let me go now."

I was becoming rather bored, and it was getting late. This needed to be sped up.

I made eye contact with Henley, who dipped his chin in acknowledgment. He bent to grab the handle on one of the buckets, then Austin stepped forward, pulling the cloth back over Chase's mouth. Chase shouted, the sound muffled by the fabric, as Henley came up behind him.

He lifted the bucket in the air, and then a gush of water was cascading over Chase's body in a rush. His gag quickly became soaked, his breaths sputtering as his hair lay damp in his eyes. Austin left the cloth like that for a moment before yanking it down again, the act anything but gentle.

A bored sigh escaped me. "Why would you need to hide?"

Chase blinked rapidly, heaving breaths. "My boss. I owe my boss."

I raised my brow the slightest bit. "What do you owe him?"

Chase tried to wipe his cheek on his shoulder, then said, "That's none of your fucking business."

"Alright." If that's how he wanted to play, I'd fucking play.

Hooking the revolver in my jeans, I walked over to the forge and withdrew the poker with my gloved hand. The fabric was heat resistant, but unfortunately for Chase, his skin wasn't. I ambled over to where Chase sat, the tip of the metal glowing bright red.

"What are you doing with that?" His words hurried, stumbling over one another.

I stopped directly in front of him. "Getting answers." The spot singed as soon as I brought the blazing tip to his flesh, eliciting a hiss as his skin melted beneath the smoldering metal. He yelled out, sweat dripping from every pore on his body.

I held it there, almost tempted to not remove it until the tool cooled. After a few seconds, I pulled it away, some of his skin coming with it. "You want to talk now? Or should I heat it up again?"

"You're fucking sick!" he yelled, slouched forward slightly now as he panted.

"You want to talk about sick?" I lifted his chin with the tip of the poker, his skin instantly singeing. He screamed, but I kept it steady. "Real fucking bold of you to sling that at me when you were the one sleeping around behind Brynne's back like a fucking coward."

I needed to get back on track, to find the deed before I put this poker through his goddamn neck, but I was losing my patience, and I didn't have much to begin with.

Tears fell down Chase's cheeks, and I removed the tool. He hung his head, saliva dripping from his mouth. "I don't owe him anymore," he managed to get out, his voice hoarse from screaming.

I walked back to the forge, laying the tool back inside, then faced him again. Henley and Austin stood by, waiting for my instruction.

"What do you mean, 'you don't owe him anymore?'" I hoped like hell he didn't mean what I thought he meant.

He sniffled, not lifting his head. "I gave him the deed this morning."

To my right, Henley's fists clenched, and on my other side, Austin cursed under his breath.

"Where can we find him?" I asked.

Chase shook his head. "You can't."

He clearly underestimated us.

"Why don't you leave that part up to us and tell me where we can find him?"

Chase was silent a moment, clearly thinking over his next words carefully. "He does his dealings at the park near the truck stop about two miles down the exit off seventy-sixth."

That was all I needed.

I gestured to Austin and Henley, who nodded in response. Grabbing Chase's gun from my waist, I aimed it straight at his chest, not giving myself a moment to breathe before pulling the trigger. The bullet landed right where his heart was, and Chase slumped forward further, his breathing ceased.

Blood poured from the wound, staining his clothes, and then, the ground. We could frame it as a suicide if we truly wanted to, a man so lovesick over his lost lover that he couldn't live without her, but the burn marks would be suspicious. Getting rid of his body wouldn't be a problem, anyway. We were well-versed in making someone disappear.

I set the gun on the shelf, pulling the glove off my hand to lay next to it in case they needed to pick it up. Then, I crossed to Chase's hunched frame, fishing around in his pockets for his cell phone. Grabbing the device, I headed out of the barn, leaving Austin and Henley to clean up the mess. The idiot didn't even have a passcode. I found the contact labeled "boss" and shot them a text, asking them to meet Chase at the exact location he had given before I lodged a bullet in his heart. Of course, it wouldn't be Chase arriving, though. It'd be his worst fucking nightmare.

Pocketing the phone, I aimed for the house, spotting the light still on upstairs.

I had other business to take care of tonight.

CHAPTER 17

BRYNNE

When I'd arrived here days ago, I'd unpacked my luggage, stuffing my few belongings in the drawers and closet. The idea that I'd be here long enough to need to do that was ridiculous, and now, as I piled all the clothing back into my two bags, I wished I would've just left them in there neatly folded away to begin with.

Maybe it would've hurt less if I had.

I shouldn't have allowed myself to grow attached. But *fuck*. Booker handled me the way I'd always wanted to be handled, like a flower that could withstand being plucked, picked, and cut. My exterior walls hid the delicateness of my heart, and he'd penetrated them with ease. He challenged me, breaking down my barriers and building them up at the same time.

And yet he'd said he wouldn't care what happened to me after all of this.

The man truly was selfish.

I should've known to never get involved with a rancher.

The land would always be more important. I'd never be a priority, and he'd made that clear.

So I zipped the luggage, hefting it up off the ground, and rolled it next to the door to finish filling the second one.

With my back to the door, I heard it creak open, but I didn't need to turn around to know who stood there. His presence dominated all the air in the room, the universe and my senses bending to him.

No footsteps sounded, indicating he was still standing in the doorway, most likely staring at my luggage.

He got what he wanted. Chase would lead him to wherever the deed was, so my part in this was over.

"What was the gunshot?" I asked, folding my green crewneck to lay it in the bag.

"Taking care of a problem." The low timbre of his voice vibrated through me, and I wanted to turn to him. I wanted so badly for him to hold me. But he wasn't like that. He was Booker—closed off and the definition of an asshole. And me? Well, I wasn't his.

I didn't respond as I shoved my socks in the side pocket of the bag.

I didn't hear him move, but then his hands were at my waist, and my hands froze on the t-shirt I was about to pick up.

"Guess what, Darlin'?" His lips were a caress on my ear, and I didn't want them to leave.

My hand fisted in the fabric as I waited for him to go on.

"He's dead, and I'm still here."

I subtly shook my head, my breaths getting shorter as my lungs tightened.

"I still care," he said, the words almost a whisper as his hands slid down to my hips, gripping them.

"Clearly you don't have your deed back, then." Otherwise, he'd be kicking me out tonight.

"No, I don't."

"So once you get it, I'm gone." I said it as if he hadn't made the rules himself. As if he didn't ingrain them in my mind earlier today.

"You're mad at me." There was no question in his tone.

"You told me you didn't care what happened to me after all of this was done." I was just his fucking pawn.

He spun me around, hands fisted in my loose sweater. "I said that to get your ass back in the truck."

"You said it because it's true," I corrected. "It's clear you don't feel anything for me, so excuse me for getting caught up in the moment."

He pulled me closer, my chest to his. "You're the only woman I do fucking feel for, Brynne, and it pisses me the fuck off."

My eyes narrowed as my teeth ground together. "Well, sorry for making you so fucking mad! I didn't ask you to fuck me, didn't ask you to be fucking nice to me, or offer for me to move in."

His fingers gripped my chin hard, tilting my head up further. I both loved and hated him for doing that in this moment, because I loved his rough hands on me, but I hated that the act fucked with my head. "You think I want you to leave after all of this?"

"Yes!" Our voices were rising, tension radiating through my limbs with the impulse to run.

"Is what I'm doing not good enough for you, then?"

His insecurities barreled into me like a freight train with no brakes. He thought I was rejecting him, that I wasn't into him. But that was the fucking problem. "What you're doing is more than enough, Booker. So much so, that I don't think I ever want to leave, because if I do, what if I never find what we have right now? What if I find another wimp like Chase or an asshole like that guy at the gym?"

His dark eyes softened, and I wanted to get lost in them. Fuck—I feared I already was.

"Then don't," he said softly.

"What?"

"Don't leave."

My mouth parted as I stared at him, studying his face like I might be able to tell if he was speaking the truth or not. Did he really want that? Want me?

"I have to." My words broke, my voice barely a whisper.

He shook his head, but rather than fight me, beg me, plead for me to stay, he showed me how desperately he needed it. Needed me. His lips crashed to mine, stealing all coherent thoughts and emotions. My feelings poured into him like a tidal wave, our mouths moving in sync as the kiss deepened. His tongue was lost, searching for salvation with mine as a galaxy of doubt washed away on the wind, leaving only us in this room with the world fading away.

The deed, Chase, the attacks—none of it mattered right now.

Only us, and the way he lifted me, my legs wrapping around his waist like they were meant to be there.

He laid me gently on the bed, hovering over me as his mouth stayed glued to mine. His hips rested between my legs, adding pressure right where I needed it. Needed him.

Reluctantly, he pulled back, standing again. I propped up on my elbows, ready to beg him to stay, but then he was pulling his shirt off, and I nearly fell back to the mattress. For the second time, I drank in the sight of tattoos and scars that littered his torso, every inch of him hard and well-defined.

He got to work on his button and zipper, dropping his jeans and boxers to the ground. His cock sprang out, and my mouth salivated at the sight. I sat up, tugging my sweater over my head. I wasn't wearing a bra, and Booker clearly loved it as his gaze heated at the sight of my bare breasts. I slid to the edge of the bed, then off the side, landing on my knees on the rug.

He grabbed my chin in his punishing grip, making me look up at him. "I want to pleasure you tonight."

"This will." I scooted forward slightly, wrapping a hand around his length. "Please."

His chest rose with his deep inhale as he debated letting me have what I wanted. "Please what, Darlin'?"

I brought my mouth to the tip of his cock, not wrapping my lips around it, as I said, "Please let me suck your cock, Booker."

His fingers tightened on my chin before his thumb rubbed my skin. "That what you want, Darlin'? To choke on my cock?"

I nodded, darting my tongue out to wet my lips and coasting it over the bead of moisture building on his head.

"Then open that pretty mouth."

I did, and he dropped my chin to thrust forward, using no restraint as he stuffed my mouth full of his cock, the tip sliding down my throat on the first go. My tongue twitched, and he tangled a hand in my hair, pulling my mouth off of him. Using his other hand, he stuck his fingers in my mouth, hooking them on the back of my tongue. I gagged, my eyes watering as he kept his digits still.

"Breathe through your nose, Darlin'. You're taking all of it tonight."

I tried to steady my breaths as he shoved his fingers deeper. Saliva dripped from my mouth as I choked, and he pulled them out fast. In a flash, he replaced his hand with his cock, keeping my head in place as he buried himself down my throat.

I did as he said, breathing through my nose to try to calm the reflex. He pulled my mouth off of him all the way, watching as my spit glistened over my chin, my eyes full of unshed tears from the fullness of him.

"You're such a good little slut." His hand caressed my cheek, and I leaned into it slightly as I caught my breath. "Always taking me so well. All your holes were made for me, weren't they?"

I nodded, and then his fist tightened in my hair as he brought his cock to my lips again. They parted, and he slid in, fucking my mouth. He used me for his own pleasure, and with that, my core heated. I was a fucking mess, on my face and between my thighs, and already, I wanted to let go.

The room was full of his groans and the sounds my mouth made as he thrust in and out of me. Each time he hit the back of my throat, I tried to hold back my gag, but every few times, my tongue would react, jumping up at the underside of his cock.

His hand reached down to my breast, squeezing the flesh in his grip. Then, his fingers moved to tug at my nipple, and pure bliss coursed through me at the sensation.

He seated his cock deep in the back of my throat again, then pulled out. He hooked his hands under my arms and lifted me, setting me on the bed. His fingers curled around the hem of my leggings before he yanked them down. He left my underwear on, but rather than shoving it to the side, he grabbed a pocket knife from his discarded pants and ripped a hole clean through the material, revealing my soaked center.

He tossed the knife to the side and dragged a finger up my pussy, his skin instantly coated. Hovering over me with a hand on the mattress, he brought the digits to my lips and I sucked them willingly.

"Taste how sweet you are, Darlin'. How good you taste when you want nothing other than me to fill you. Fuck you. Please you."

He popped his finger out of my mouth, then brought it back to my pussy. He slid two into my entrance, and I arched my back, a moan escaping my lips.

His lips clamped down on my nipple, pulling it into his mouth with a hard suck. His tongue darted along the bud, his teeth grazing it, sending electricity sparking through my very veins. He lit me like a goddamn light bulb, and I never wanted to be turned off. This feeling was all I ever wanted, and I could die happy at his hands in this moment.

His fingers thrust in and out fast, the tips of them hooked just enough to hit that perfect spot deep inside me.

My head tossed back, exposing my neck. His mouth released my breast, and I instantly missed him as he removed the digits as well.

Right as I opened my eyes to look up at him, he was placing my vibrator against my clit and clicking it on. Stars burst in my vision as he wrapped a large hand around my throat, pressing me into the bed. He added pressure, cutting off my air as my lower back arched the slightest bit. He watched my reaction as he clicked up the speed, the toy bringing me close to the edge I so desperately wanted to fall off of.

His hand lifted slightly, staying on my throat but giving me enough reprieve to allow me to breathe. I sucked in air, but all too quickly, he was cutting it off again, and my belly twitched as my orgasm rushed through me without warning.

My thighs clenched together as butterflies swarmed my insides, lighting every nerve on fire and cooling it with ice all at the same time. Booker let me breathe again as I released, and my scream rent through the air as he kept the toy on my clit.

My body shook, my thighs tense, as wave after wave rippled through me in every which way. Then, he removed his hand, setting it on the bed beside my head, and kept the vibrator on my clit as he slid his cock inside me. My orgasm peaked again with the feeling of him filling me.

"You're so fucking tight after you come," Booker hissed, moving his hips.

I moaned, the sound filling the room as he quickened his thrusts. He brought his hand around my neck again, cutting off my windpipe as he fucked me.

There was no holding back, no dodging our feelings. We were one and the same in this moment, and I wanted nothing else more than this.

He groaned before seating himself to the hilt, spilling inside me as my release kept coming. He slid the vibrator out from between us, clicking it off and tossing it to the comforter as he lightened his hold on my neck. I sucked in air as we stayed together, and when I looked up at him, I found him staring at me.

He removed his hand altogether, setting both on either side of my head. Booker dipped down, pressing a gentle kiss to my lips. Then, he rolled off the side of me, wrapping his arms around my body to pull me closer to him. I rested my head on his tattooed chest, laying a leg over his muscular thigh. My fingers coasted over the swirls of ink, lingering on the puckered skin where various slices had healed over the years.

We fell asleep like that, with our feelings shouted into the universe and our bodies weaving them into permanent existence.

I wouldn't be leaving, and he wouldn't send me away.

The thought both terrified and excited me all the same, but I swallowed my fear and let Booker hold me until morning.

Chapter 18

Booker

Austin picked the lock with quick efficiency, getting us into the dark house in minutes. Cigarette smoke and a metallic tang stuck to the stuffy air, and with a glance at the kitchen counter, a long-forgotten cigarette butt had small tendrils of smoke rising from an ash-ridden dish.

Each window had black-out curtains covering them, making it hard to see much of anything, but we didn't turn on any lights as we dispersed. The meet-up spot wasn't too far from here, and once he found out Chase wasn't there, he'd turn straight around. I didn't take him to be a dumb man, so I was sure he'd catch on the moment he arrived.

Austin took the small office in the front entry while Henley checked all the other drawers in the house. That left me to the two bedrooms down the hall. One was completely empty save for a black tarp on the ground, and the other held a bed, dresser, and a nightstand. I would've thought that a person such as him would have more to his name, but this could very well be a temporary home, one he stayed in when he came into town to collect, or by the looks of the other room, to take care of business.

I rifled through the nightstand drawer, finding nothing but a box of condoms, then moved to lift the mattress. I was careful to put everything back how I found it, and the others were doing the same. We wanted to leave no trace we were here, and in case he had cameras, we wore all black aside from our skeleton masks, even our cowboy hats matching the attire.

Brynne hadn't put up a fight when I asked her to stay at the ranch, and I was thankful for it. I didn't need her getting caught in the crossfire if things went haywire here. I'd already almost lost her more times than I liked, and I wouldn't risk it again.

There was only so many times I was willing to fuck with fate, and I'd reached my limit when it came to Brynne's life. Anyone else, and I wouldn't give a shit. But Brynne had ingrained herself into my mind, wrapping herself around my heart like a cocoon, and never would I have thought butterflies would flutter through my stomach at the mere thought of a woman.

Yet here I was.

Moving to the closet, I dug through a few shoeboxes from the top shelf, my gloved fingers making it difficult to look through each paper as I flipped them under the flashlight. None were the deed.

With a muffled curse, I set them back where they'd been on the shelf, careful to realign them with the lines in the dust where they'd been sitting for who knew how long.

After finishing in the closet, I surveyed the room, trying

to think where I would hide an important paper if I was the controlling man.

Right as I was about to flip up the rug, Henley announced, "Got it!"

I did a quick glance to make sure everything was in place, then headed back down the hall to find him standing in the kitchen, holding up the paper.

"Where'd you find it?" Austin asked, walking through the threshold to the office.

"Underneath the utensil tray. Stupid ass place to hide it, if you ask me," Henley said.

I approached him, taking the deed from his hand to look it over.

It was ours, that much was certain.

Austin peered over my shoulder, his eyes scanning the page. With a small nod, he said, "Alright, let's get the fuck out of here."

I quickly folded it, then froze with the paper halfway in my back pocket as a car door slammed outside.

Their eyes widened behind their masks as my heart thumped in my chest.

Fuck.

Shoving it the rest of the way in my jeans, we beelined for the back door. We had no time to figure out how to lock it behind us. We slid out right as the front door opened, disappearing from sight after quietly closing it. We didn't stick around to see if he realized we were here as we hurried around the side of the house to the narrow strip of overgrown grass leading to the back gate.

Austin jumped over the fence first, then Henley, and next, me. Once on the sidewalk, we slowed our pace, not wanting to bring attention to ourselves. We removed our masks, holding them at our sides in case any cars passed and were suspicious. Halloween was soon, though, so I was sure no one would look twice.

To my surprise, no one followed us. We made it to the truck where I got behind the wheel, Austin in the passenger seat, and Henley behind me. Dusk cast everything in shadows, but to be safe, I didn't turn the headlights on until we were out of the neighborhood.

I drove straight to the ranch, glancing at the clock. We'd arrive right at the time Brynne said she wanted us back. She had plans with McKenna to go to the haunted house tonight, and of course, Brynne was dragging the three of us along, despite knowing that wasn't our scene. After everything that happened this week, I wanted her to have fun, and I felt like I owed it to her after she stayed home for this, so I couldn't say no.

Not to her.

Not anymore.

I fucking hated the soft side of me that came out around her, like she placed cotton candy around the bloody knives and brick walls in my head, making my sharp edges have no choice but to be sweet and lose their deadly bite for her.

In minutes, I was turning down the driveway to the ranch. We pulled up, finding Brynne sitting on the front steps in leggings and a sweater. She stood as I pulled the truck to a stop, and Austin got out to let Brynne slide into the passenger seat. He closed the door, taking a seat in the back as Brynne reached over to place a kiss on my cheek.

"No costume?" I asked, making my way back to the main road as she buckled herself.

"McKenna has it. I'll just change at her house. And what are you supposed to be?" she asked, eyeing my black attire.

Turning onto the road, I grabbed the mask where it sat on the center console, holding it up for emphasis.

"How original," she said blandly.

"The mask not do it for you, Darlin'?"

She shifted on the seat, and with a glance her way, I noticed the apples of her cheeks were now stained pink.

A smirk held the side of my mouth as I drove to McKenna's house, following Brynne's directions. Once there, Brynne hopped out to run inside and change. She hadn't told me what her costume would be. Every time I asked, she'd get quiet, almost like she was embarrassed.

And when she emerged from the peeling-paint door, why she may have been ashamed to tell me became all too apparent.

She was dressed up as a slutty cowgirl, and the way those little jean shorts barely covered the tops of her thighs did things to me I didn't want to admit.

Never in my life would I think I'd be adjusting myself over a costume-induced boner.

McKenna locked the door, then headed down the narrow pathway to the truck. From the looks of it, she was dressed as a rated-R Barbie.

With her lips a thin line, Brynne scooted onto the passenger seat as Austin moved to the middle in the back, allowing McKenna to slide in beside him. One glance in the rearview mirror told me exactly how Austin felt about her little costume as his eyes roamed over every inch of her. McKenna seemed to enjoy it as she puffed out her chest, her extremely short pink dress accentuating all of her curves. It was split up the middle, a buckle across her breasts barely keeping it together, along with a strap around her neck.

Next to me, Brynne wore a little red top that tied in the center of her cleavage, a bandana tied around her neck, a white felt cowgirl hat that had a beige band around it, and white boots. They'd be freezing, and neither had emerged with a jacket, indicating they didn't care. If need be, Brynne could wear my sweatshirt, and I was sure Austin would be more than willing to offer up his own to McKenna.

"Shots, anyone?" McKenna asked, her voice airy and sweet, hinting at the possibility of her already having drank a few. She dug through her little purse, pulling out a couple bottles of fireball.

My nose burned at the thought.

"I'll pass," I grumbled as Henley and Austin eagerly took one each from her. McKenna passed one up to Brynne as well.

I watched as she uncapped it, then kept her eyes on me as she downed the entire thing in one gulp, her pink lips wrapping around the top. I hated fireball, but fuck me for wanting to know what it tasted like on her tongue. As soon as the last drop left the bottle and her face scrunched from the alcohol, I wrapped a hand around the back of her neck, making her lean over the center console to press her lips to mine. I darted my tongue into her mouth, lapping up the cinnamon flavor mixed with her sweet, minty taste. I could've gotten drunk off this alone.

Satisfied with the flavor that now bounced around in

my own mouth, I let her settle back in her seat, then shifted into drive to head toward the haunted house. It sat on the outskirts of town, right at the peak of Whiskey Hill. It was the tallest point in all of town, hence it taking part of the name. I didn't believe the place was actually haunted. The county most likely started the rumors themselves to make money off people wanting to run around an old, abandoned house with the thought of ghosts or other eerie things following them.

It was all a gimmick, but Brynne and her best friend wanted to go, so we'd entertain it only for tonight—to let loose after the shit week we'd all had.

Once Chase's boss inevitably figured out the deed was missing, I was sure he'd come looking for it, but there was no way I'd let it go a second time. He'd have to kill all three of us and pry it from our cold, lifeless hands if he wanted it.

The parking lot for the haunted house was nearly full, so I parked the truck at the back of the lot, hoping it'd be easier to leave once we were done here. Turning off the engine, we all got out, then headed toward the line leading into the attraction.

"I bought all our tickets beforehand," McKenna said, pulling her phone out of her handbag as we stopped at the end of the line.

Brynne stood beside me, and I glanced down at her, not sure how to go about being in public together. I'd never really had an official girlfriend, always just on and off flings. But Brynne was clearly more. Hell, if she wasn't, she would be. I wasn't letting her go.

Lacing my hand into hers, I turned her so her back was to my chest, then I wrapped an arm around her shoulders.

Her hand stayed in mine, and I ran a thumb along her skin. It felt nice to not have the pressure of getting the deed back anymore, or dealing with her ex, or a target on her back—for the time being. Tonight, we could have fun.

It was something I hadn't allowed myself to do in a long time.

The ranch always came first. Keeping it afloat assured me, Henley, and Austin that we'd have a place to live. We worked hard, earned every penny to get where we were today, and I wouldn't let that be pulled out from under us so easily.

Now, I had a girl to share it with. One who unexpectedly came into my life and opened my heart under scalpel and knife, inserting herself into it without even knowing.

A few minutes later, we approached the front of the line, and a man scanned the barcode lit up on McKenna's phone, allowing us entry. The five of us walked up the steep hill, approaching the tall, open doors that entered into darkness. Screams rent through the air from the inside, people presumably jumping out from behind hidden corners and scaring their friends.

We stopped in front of the entrance, staring up at the house that loomed before us like hell itself. Pieces of wood had fallen off in various places, proving it was unstable in and of itself. Black paint peeled off the shutters, windows were shattered, and a decaying smell wafted out from the inside, stinging my nostrils.

With an arm looped around Brynne's waist, I ran a hand down her forearm, feeling the goosebumps that peppered her skin from the cold.

"If you're scared, we can always take this back to the

ranch," I murmured in her ear. I could elicit the same thrill they were seeking here. I was sure Austin wouldn't mind having his fun with McKenna, either.

Brynne swallowed, shaking her head as a couple passed us. "No. We always go in, don't we, McKenna?"

McKenna flicked her attention to her best friend. "Every year."

With that, Austin, Henley, and I situated our masks on our faces, then we stepped over the threshold. The wooden beam creaked under our combined weight, and then we were thrust into darkness.

CHAPTER 19

BRYNNE

I thought being inside the creepy house would be a bit warmer than outside, but I was sorely mistaken. If anything, the air seemed to drop ten degrees just stepping inside the door. Wearing such a revealing outfit wasn't the smartest thing to do in the northern Idaho fall weather, but McKenna had insisted. I had the biggest feeling she planned our costumes as such because she wanted one of the guys to give her their sweatshirt. With the way Austin stayed close behind her, a hand ghosting her waist, I wouldn't doubt he'd be offering soon. Booker, on the other hand, would wait until I asked. Internally, I knew he'd give it up without question, but he wasn't the kind of guy who would outright ask if I wanted it, and I liked that about him. So many of my ex-boyfriends would be weird if I wore their clothes, or they'd force it onto me when I didn't actually want them. But Booker demanded, and already, he took care of me when he knew I needed it.

"Let's go to the basement first," McKenna said, leading

us toward the staircase that, upon first look, led to nothing but a pit of black.

"We usually hit there last," I reminded her. We avoided it in the beginning because it was no secret that all the couples went down there to find dark corners to make out in. If we waited until last, they'd typically cleared out by then, taking their flaming hormones elsewhere.

McKenna wagged her eyebrows. "Let's change it up this year."

Her eager smile made me all too aware of what she was thinking.

I looked up at Booker, who was watching our surroundings from behind his mask, surveying the people that ran every which way all around us, seeking their next thrill.

"The basement okay?" I asked him.

His dark eyes moved to me. "Anywhere you want, Darlin'. We're following you tonight."

A slight zing zipped through my body at the fact that they were taking my direction. I wanted to do more than just lead them around a scary house, but this would have to suffice. For now.

We headed toward the top of the stairs, and as we did, McKenna called out, "Grace!"

All our heads swiveled to the right, landing on McKenna's cousin. Grace was wearing a revealing Playboy bunny costume, a pair of ears and a tiny ball of fluff above her ass completing the look.

Her face lit up when she saw us, one of the few flickering candle lights casting dancing shadows over the man she had on her arm.

"McKenna!" Grace shrieked, tugging the tall blonde our way.

"How are things?" McKenna asked, a huge grin pulling at her mouth.

I glanced between the two of them, then sent an apologetic half-smile to Booker as McKenna and Grace began babbling about work and who the tall drink of water was on Grace's arm. The man didn't look too happy to be here, but I guessed that was normal considering the three guys with us most likely had similar expressions hidden behind their masks.

"Oh my gosh, you guys go on without me," McKenna said, turning her attention back to me for a split second with a wave of her hand.

"Are you sure? We can wait." I didn't feel the most comfortable leaving her.

McKenna nodded, her high-pony bobbing. "Yes, I'm sure! I'll find you guys down there."

I hated going on without her, but I also knew the guys didn't want to be here long, and being as McKenna and I had already been through this place dozens of times, I figured we could make quick work of exploring the basement, then head back up to find her still here talking.

"Okay. Call me if you can't find us," I said.

She nodded, then went back to chatting with Grace.

I tested each step with the toe of my cowgirl boot before continuing down the stairs with the guys in tow. The staircase was narrow, allowing only single formation on the way down. The air grew colder and almost denser as moisture coated the space. All the while my body shivered, my hand stayed warm where it was gripped in Booker's behind me.

We reached the bottom, only having the option to go one way or the other as we faced a cinder block wall. A candle was lit, held by a gothic black sconce, providing our only source of light as I steered us down the right hall.

We approached a corner, and right when I went to round it, a man jumped out wearing a red steampunk mask with little spikes darting out of it. I jumped back, straight into Booker's chest, where he grabbed hold of my upper arms. The guy stuck his tongue out as he growled, then ran past us, out of sight. My heart thumped in my chest as I caught my breath.

"Scared, Darlin'?" Booker murmured in my ear.

"Yes." There was no lying. Every year, the same adrenaline of walking around this place in the dark coursed through me, and every year, I was scared when things jumped out at us—as if I wasn't already expecting it.

"Good."

Then my hat was being shucked off, and a bag was thrown over my head. My scream was muffled in the scratchy fabric as I was lifted off the ground. His strong grip kept my arms to my sides as he carried me somewhere, but I didn't struggle.

Instead, my skin hummed in anticipation.

———

My arms were tied above my head with the bag still blocking my view from what was going on around me. All I could hear were footsteps and their deep breathing as they strung me up. It'd been minutes since we were in the hall, and the only indication that we were now in a room was a door closing behind us before one of them bound me.

The bag was removed, but little light penetrated my eyes in the dark room. A single candle flickered in the space, faintly illuminating the three men in front of me. Their masks covered their faces, but familiarity coursed over me, giving me slight comfort. I was safe, and yet, the thrill of what was to come wracked my body.

"I think it's time Henley had his fun, don't you?" Booker asked, turning his head to Austin. The three of them all wore black cowboy hats, looking nearly identical under the disguises.

Austin kept his gaze locked on me, and behind the mask, I saw his eyes heat. "I think so."

Booker approached me, stopping directly in front of me where I stood in the center of the room. My arms were pulled taught, my body on display, save for the little bit of clothing I wore. He grabbed my chin, searching my face. "Are you going to be a good little slut for my friend, Darlin'?"

I nodded.

His fingers gripped my chin harder. "Use your words like a good girl, and maybe I won't punish you for keeping that mouth shut."

I rolled my lips together, debating if I should obey. I'd listened to everything he demanded of me thus far, and tonight, I wanted to see what happened if I didn't. I shook my head.

Booker's eyes were twin flames of charcoal as he moved

his hand from my chin to my neck in a flash, squeezing my windpipe shut.

I had no time to inhale before he cut my breathing off, and my lips parted as I tried to suck in air. His other hand pulled my tiny crop-top down past one of my breasts, exposing the flesh. He brought his hand back, slapping my breast. The sting flowed through me, along with the burn of my lungs.

"What about now, Darlin'? You want to be a good girl and listen? Or do I need to teach you a lesson and treat you like the bad little slut that you are?"

He eased the pressure on my neck ever so slightly, and I gasped in air, my lungs screaming for more.

Still, I didn't speak. I wanted him to punish me. To push me to my limits while I was completely at their mercy.

I shook my head.

He yanked down the other side of my shirt, sending a stinging slap to my opposite breast. Then, he was moving his hand to my hair, yanking my head back so my tits were forced forward more, my neck exposed.

"Henley." Steps sounded on the cement floor, and then Booker was speaking again. "Suck on her tits."

In less than a second, a mouth was clamped down on my nipple, sucking it hard. Henley had shoved his mask up slightly and was lapping his tongue around the bud while he gripped my breast in his hand.

Booker tugged my hair harder, bringing his masked face closer to mine. "That what you want, Brynne? The three of us pleasuring you?"

I nodded, despite his hold on me.

But my silence only drove him forward.

"Austin," he boomed.

More footsteps, and then Austin was beside me.

"Show her what happens when she doesn't obey."

Behind his mask, a smirk rent his mouth, and then he disappeared from my sight. My shorts were ripped down my legs, my tiny thong along with them, and then he was sending a slap against my clit, and my body jerked. The rope burned my wrists, but I didn't care. I wanted them to keep going.

Booker released my hair as Austin thrust two fingers inside me without warning. I let out a yelp as Henley bit down on my nipple. Booker stepped back, watching as they both wracked me with pleasure.

"My little slut likes the attention, doesn't she?" Booker groaned. I could see his boner aching to be free, and I wanted nothing more than to feel him inside me. I tried to nod in response, but every nerve in my body homed in on the way Austin and Henley played with me, making it near impossible to focus.

Booker must've seen the look on my face, because he took one large step towards me and reached up. My arms fell as he took the rope off the hook, and Henley's mouth left my breast as he stepped back. Austin removed his fingers, and then Booker was pulling me to the ground on top of him. He reached between us, freeing his cock at the same time Henley grabbed my tied hands and held them up.

"Open," Henley instructed, and I realized his cock was out, directly in front of my face.

I glanced down at Booker, who nodded his approval. I

was only okay with any of this if he was, and his unspoken words gave me the courage to open my mouth.

Henley slid his cock past my lips at the same time Booker filled my pussy with his length. Booker's hands dug into my waist, holding me steady as he thrust in and out of me.

With Henley's grip on the rope holding my arms up, he fucked my mouth, causing saliva to drip down my chin and along my neck. Then, pressure filled me from behind, and I realized Austin was sliding a wet finger in my ass.

Every ounce of friction in all three of my holes brought me closer to release. My breasts swung directly in front of Booker's face, and he watched with rapt attention as he continued to slide in and out of me at a punishing pace.

Austin's finger disappeared from my ass, and then cool liquid slid down the hole as something larger was replacing it, and I realized it was his cock. Henley pulled out just in time for my scream to fill the air. Austin was huge, bigger than anything I'd ever felt back there, and between him and Booker, I felt beyond full.

"You can take it, little slut," Booker reassured, slowing his pace.

Austin set a hand on my back, sliding deeper. "Relax, Brynne. Just like that."

Henley's eyes darted around my face as Austin settled further inside me, and I moaned, trying my best to relax around him.

"I-I can't—"

"You can," Booker demanded. "Breathe, Darlin'. You're taking all of us."

I looked down at him as he paused his thrusts altogether. Austin seated himself to the hilt, running a reassuring hand over my ass. I adjusted to the size of him, my heaving breaths making my chest rise and fall. Austin let his spit fall between us, and then he was slowly pulling out again.

Booker resumed thrusting in and out of my pussy as Austin matched his pace. Henley gripped his shaft, repositioning it in front of my mouth.

"Only if you want to," Henley said hesitantly.

I nodded up at him and parted my lips. He slid in, and Booker's thumb praised me as it stroked my side.

"You look so fucking good taking all three of us," Booker groaned as the two of them picked up their pace.

Henley hit the back of my throat and I gagged, my eyes watering on instinct. He slid out slowly, then did it again, and again.

One of Booker's hands wrapped around my breast, squeezing. "Just like how I taught you, little slut."

My throat hummed around Henley's cock as Austin fucked my ass relentlessly. They filled every part of me, and my body was on fire with the feeling of them. It was overwhelming and a welcome blissful sensation all at the same time, and I wanted to rupture.

Henley pulled out again, pumping his cock. "Can I come in your mouth, Brynne?"

I glanced down at Booker again. He was in charge, and I'd gladly let him make the decisions.

Booker nodded, releasing my breast to wrap a rough hand around my throat. Henley took that as his answer.

Henley slid past my swollen lips, fucking my mouth as hard as Booker and Austin were thrusting. Booker squeezed my neck, cutting off my breath as Henley continued hitting the back of my throat. With a groan, warmth spurted across my tongue, coating me. I swallowed every last drop after Booker relaxed his hand. Henley's hold on the rope slackened slightly, my elbows bending with the act.

Booker took that as his cue and hooked his hands under my armpits, bringing me down as Henley dropped the rope. My hands were still tied as Booker placed them on his chest, their thrusts insistent.

Behind me, Austin spanked my ass at the same time Booker set a thumb on my clit, rubbing circles around the bud. I gasped at the pressure building in my core, and then my muscles tightened, my thighs gripping Booker's hips as I let go. Austin and Booker quickened their pace as I released around them, my body shaking with their cocks filling me.

Right when I thought I was coming down from my orgasm, another wracked through me as Booker increased the pressure on my clit. I screamed, Booker's name a curse on my lips as my legs shook.

Then, Austin let out a groan, and he seated himself deep inside me. Warmth filled me soon after as Booker did the same. With the two of them as deep as they could go, I almost felt pressure build for a third time. Booker could tell, and his thumb made hard circles on my sensitive bud, and then I was shaking again. The room filled with my moans as I fell to his chest, panting and shaking.

Slowly, Austin slid out from behind me, and then it was just me and Booker. He held me, letting my breathing return to normal and the shaking to stop flowing through my limbs. While my lungs heaved, Austin came over to untie the rope around my wrists, and then Henley was there, running lotion along the abrasions.

I sat up slightly, eying him. "Thank you."

He gave me a short nod, and one glance at the two of them told me they'd already cleaned themselves up and situated their pants.

As soon as Henley was done rubbing in the lotion, I sat up straighter, looking down at Booker. His eyes glistened in the candlelight as he stared up at me, his hand running a slow circle on my hip.

We held each other, mentally and physically, in that moment, and what I saw in his gaze couldn't be what I thought it was, but the realization hit me all the same.

Booker felt a lot more for me than I originally thought.

Blinking, I moved to get up, and he shoved up on his elbows to help me stand. He was beside me in a flash, pulling off his sweatshirt. "Wear this."

Before I could take it from him, he was pulling it over my head, helping lead my arms through the sleeves. It was huge on me.

As I pulled my hair out of the neckline, he handed me my shorts and thong, and I slid them on. The sweatshirt covered them, but it was a lot warmer than what I'd had on before. Reaching up underneath, I fixed my breasts back into my top as Booker ran a thumb along my chin, wiping away the lingering saliva.

"I should go find McKenna," I said, realizing that she wouldn't have found us even if she did go looking.

Booker grabbed my hand. "I'll come with while they clean up here."

I frowned at him. "You have your friends fuck your girl and then make them do the cleanup?"

The reality that I'd just called myself his girl hit the both of us at the same time. His thumb grazed the side of my hand in response.

"Looks like it," he said.

I shook my head. "Nuh-uh. You help them. I think I can handle finding my best friend on my own. I feel kind of bad that I ditched her."

He tugged me toward him, our chests pressed together. "She told us to go ahead."

"Yeah, well, that doesn't mean I don't feel guilty for it. We do this together every year, and now she's up there alone while I'm down here with the three of you."

"She could've joined," Austin said from the other side of the room.

I moved my gaze to him, and in doing so, I saw the mess we'd made on the ground. Wetness stained the cement in odd places, and the rope laid on the ground in a heap beside the bag that had been over my head.

"You guys need to figure this out," I gestured to the floor. "I'll be fine."

Booker forced my face back to him with a gentle hand on my cheek, and I realized he'd lifted his mask. He pressed his lips to mine, our mouths mending together as he laced his fingers in my hair.

As we parted, something was placed on my head, and I reached a hand up to find Henley had given me my cowgirl hat back.

I pulled away from Booker, backing toward the door. "Meet us upstairs, okay?"

Booker nodded, pulling his mask back down. I turned around, wrapping a hand around the knob and opening the creaky door. I slipped out, closing it behind me so no one would hopefully go in there while they somehow took care of what we'd done.

As I headed down the dark hall, I bit my lip with the memory of how all three of them had made me feel. I'd never felt anything as fulfilling as that, but my mind went back to Booker—how he'd looked up to me with admiration, like I was the only one in his universe.

He was having the same effect on me, and I wanted to embrace it. When I left Chase, I hadn't felt heartbroken, which was why when Booker told me they'd killed him, I hadn't flinched. Chase was an asshole, digging himself into a hole that would've ended up with him dead anyway. Booker just sped up the process.

I rounded the corner, but as I did, a hand clamped down on my arm, pulling me back. I spun, expecting to find Booker or one of the others, but before I could get a good look, something hit me hard on the side of the head, and I fell forward into stiff arms, and my vision went black.

CHAPTER 20

BOOKER

My eyes were glued to the door where Brynne had just disappeared. She hadn't acted ashamed or phased by what had happened between the four of us. She'd been so willing to take us at the same time, so eager to let us have our way with her. And the sight of her afterward—in *my* sweatshirt, with my cum still deep inside her pussy—made me absolutely awestruck.

While I was nothing but amazed at how well she took us, I had a feeling deep in my core that I didn't ever want to share her again. She was slowly becoming mine, and I was quickly wanting to claim her as such.

"She's not going to reappear," Austin grumbled behind me, and I turned to find him standing there with his hands on his hips, the rope gripped in one fist.

Henley was staring at the dark spot on the ground before snapping his head toward me. "It's not like I brought fucking wet wipes to clean the concrete."

"Just do something with the rope and bag and shit, in case anyone gets any ideas and decides to kill someone with them tonight. Last thing I need is a murder planted on me."

Austin frowned. "As if you don't already have multiple that are on your hands?"

I reciprocated the look. "You two aren't innocent either."

I stepped forward, bending over to snag the burlap bag off the slab of cement. I wanted the fuck out of this muggy room with these two and to be back by Brynne's side.

An image of her tied up with the bag loose over her head flashed through my mind, and my jeans felt all too tight again.

"Miss her already?" Austin asked, rolling the rope up as he watched me.

I cleared my throat, heading for the door with the scratchy material tight in my fist. "No, asshole."

"I think he's lying," Austin mumbled to Henley, who muttered his agreement.

I tore the door open a little too hard, stepping out in the hall right as a child ran by with a teenager on her heels, the two girls screaming as they darted down the narrow walkway.

Austin and Henley were behind me, and the telltale sound of a thud muffled through the tight space as Austin got rid of the rope on our way. At the bottom of the staircase, I did the same, tossing the bag to the side before we headed up the confined stairs. Once we emerged from the musty basement, the air felt lighter, but still, the hairs on the back of my neck stood straight.

I searched the room for Brynne, but I found McKenna instead. We crossed the space to her where she was still talking to Grace. It was a wonder they had this many things to talk about, but knowing what I did about McKenna, I was sure she could go all night if given the opportunity.

Both girls pinned their eyes on us as we approached.

"Hey, guys!" McKenna greeted. At some point, Grace's date must've ditched her, because he was nowhere in sight.

My eyes scanned the entryway and open area to our right, finding no sign of Brynne.

"Is Brynne with you?" I asked.

"She's not with you guys?"

My head snapped to her. "No. She came up here to find you."

A small furrow crested McKenna's brows as a confused expression crossed her face. "She must still be looking, then—"

But I didn't stick around to hear what she had to say. Brynne knew exactly where we'd left McKenna, which would've been the first place she looked. If she wasn't here, then she wasn't in the house, period.

"It's okay. It's not your fault." Austin's falsely soothing voice sounded as he presumably reassured McKenna, but it wasn't okay. Brynne could be gone or worse—

If anyone hurt my girl, I'd gut the fucker who thought he could get away with it. Rip his sternum wide open and remove organ after organ while he begged for mercy.

But that's where he'd fucked up big time.

I didn't grant mercy to those who took what was mine.

I rid them of every bloody piece inside them, the thing that kept them living, because that's what it felt like in this moment, not knowing where Brynne was.

Like my goddamned heart was torn clean from my chest.

Along with the hope that maybe she was caught up in a conversation with a friend. Or outside getting some air.

Because I knew the feeling all too fucking well when the devil was out to play.

"Booker," Henley called out to me as I took the basement stairs two at a time.

As soon as I reached the bottom, my head swiveled both ways, and on the second glance down the way we'd come from, I froze. The bandana that had been around Brynne's neck lay in a bundle on the floor. I crossed the three feet to it, grabbing the material in a fist. If I wasn't already certain something had happened to her, I was now.

Turning the opposite way, I went down the way we hadn't been before. My shoulders brushed the cold walls as my boots echoed on the cement. She had to be down here. She fucking had to be.

"Booker!" Henley called again, but I wouldn't fucking stop. Not until I found her.

The first door I came upon, I slammed it open, the wood crashing against the wall so hard it splintered. A couple making out broke apart, frantic eyes jumping to me. With no sign of her, I moved on.

For the next three doors, I did the same, either finding them empty or with two horny people trying to find privacy in this house of horrors.

A strong hand grabbed my shoulder, but I shrugged it off. Not even a second later, it was back, gripping my flesh hard. "Booker."

I spun, smoke practically billowing from my nose as I was two steps away from breaking Henley's goddamn hand.

He held his palms up in surrender, backing a step away. "Breathe, man."

I closed the space, getting in his face because if I couldn't take it out on whoever had her, I'd do it to the next closest person. "You think she has time to breathe right now, Henley? That whoever has her is allowing her to be calm?" Our noses touched, but he stood his ground. "No!" My voice echoed down the hall. "They probably want her scared. Want her all fucking vulnerable."

The thought alone made me fucking sick.

Brynne would only be vulnerable for me. Scared of *me*. *Swallow your fear, Darlin'. I'm coming.*

"She's not here. You're wasting your time," Henley said.

His statement had my blood turning to ice as I straightened. "How the fuck would you know?" If he had a hand in her disappearance—

"The meetup spot Chase told us about off forty-nine. If his boss is trying to lure you somewhere, he'd choose there. He clearly knows you know about it now."

It made sense. He was probably waiting there right now, and I was wasting my time searching a rotting house. Brynne took over every coherent thought in my mind, and all I could focus on right now was getting to her, but I wasn't being smart. Henley was a fucking saint.

I placed stiff palms on either side of his face, Brynne's bandana wrapped around my fingers, and shook him slightly. "You're a goddamn genius." My hands dropped, and I was slipping past him in a hurry. "Get Austin and meet me at the truck. I'm leaving with or without you."

Henley hurried after me and parted ways to grab Austin, who was lost in conversation with McKenna. By the looks of it, she was upset, and he was comforting her. They could do that sappy shit after we found Brynne. But even if Austin decided not to come, I'd still walk into the flames to find her.

Not a minute passed after I'd made it to my truck when Austin and Henley came running up to the doors to hop in. Thankfully, Austin had left McKenna with her cousin. I didn't need more people getting in the way. It'd killed me to give them those sixty seconds, but I didn't know what I was walking into when I got to the park, so having at least one of them by my side was the smart thing to do.

With the truck already started, my tires peeled out of the gravel lot, and then we were heading down the highway to the unknown, and my girl.

CHAPTER 21

BRYNNE

*S*tay quiet and don't scream. That's what he wants me to do. He wants a reaction, and I'm not going to give it to him.

My body jostled side to side in the back of what I assumed to be a vehicle. I wasn't in a seat, nor was I crammed uncomfortably in a trunk, which meant it had to be a van. I wasn't skilled in figuring out my surroundings without seeing where I was, but I had to learn real quick how to sense anything and everything with a cloth tied over my eyes.

"Wonder what she's got under that sweatshirt," a man said with a nasally voice.

A raspy chuckle sounded from my other side. "Bet her boyfriend wouldn't mind if we had a little look."

"Boss said to leave her to him," another male called back from somewhere behind me. He must be the one driving the van.

The other two had to be at least two or three feet from me, on either side of the vehicle. My hands were bound behind my back, making it hard to stay upright with each bump and turn, but I refused to lose my balance. It'd only make me look more vulnerable if I did.

I'd woken from the hit only minutes ago, and as soon as I did, I'd scrambled to this sitting position, with my back pressed firmly against the metal wall behind me. This was the first they'd spoken, and I couldn't decide if knowing they were in here with me made me feel better than the suffocating silence. To die alone or with an audience was a decision I didn't think I'd ever want to make—not that they'd let me have a say, anyway.

"Well, the boss ain't here right now, is he?" nasally guy shot back.

"We don't even need to touch her to get a show," the raspy one said, then added, "Her ass is practically spilling out of those shorts."

I swallowed hard, shifting where I sat to try to hide their view of my ass, but without being able to see, I didn't know if the position I moved into was enough to block it. I mentally cursed McKenna for making me wear this slutty cowgirl costume. I'd thought the outfit would be cute to taunt Booker with—not to end up getting eye-fucked by some creeps.

Brakes squealed as the van stopped moving, but the engine didn't turn off. Silence stretched for too long before the sound of a door opening filled the space, and the vehicle dipped slightly as someone must've gotten in.

"You listen to my instructions?" a deep, unsettling voice asked. Somehow, it seemed familiar, but I couldn't place it. I blamed the hit on my head for making me imagine things.

"Yes, boss. Got the girl in one piece, just like you asked," the nasally one answered.

"That amount of blood on her face and you think that's one piece?" the one I assumed was the boss questioned.

I folded in on myself slightly with the knowledge that there was blood on me. I hadn't realized I was that injured with my focus on where I was and who was with me. Pain was an afterthought.

"Gun nicked her head when I hit her," the raspy one said.

"I don't give a shit. Get the fuck out."

Rustling filled my ears before the van dipped again, and then the doors were shut. Behind me, the peep door must've been closed as well as a scrape sounded. But I knew I wasn't alone.

"Quiet one, aren't you?" the boss asked, but with his tone, it was clear he was taunting me, trying to get a reaction.

I wouldn't give in.

Two footfalls, and the cloth was ripped from my face. I blinked rapidly as my eyes adjusted to my surroundings. I was correct in that I was currently in a van, and by the smears of old blood on the wall, I could tell this wasn't their first time holding someone in here.

I refused to look up at the man standing before me, so I kept my gaze on the door just past him. A rough hand gripped my chin, forcing my face up, but I didn't give him my eyes. He wouldn't get the satisfaction of seeing any hint of fear in them.

"Stubborn little bitch, aren't you?"

I pressed my lips firm together as his grip tightened. Tears pooled in my eyes, but still, I wouldn't look.

"Don't make me ask, Brynne. I don't use manners."

Manners or not, he wouldn't get what he wanted.

If he was using me for bait, chances were, Booker would leave me here to die. He had his deed—he had no reason to come save me.

Our deal...it was done. And even though he'd said he was still there, a part of me still believed he was only using me for the time being. We had our moments, but was it enough to risk his life for me? His inconvenient house guest was gone, and it was just one more thing taken off his plate.

I didn't see it as the boss pulled his hand back, but I felt the sting when his palm made contact with my cheek. My head jerked to the side as I squeezed my eyes shut, but he forced it back in his direction.

"Open those eyes, bitch. Let me see your fear."

But I didn't. I swallowed that shit down like a fucking pill and acted on impulse.

My legs weren't bound, so I used the opportunity to catch him off guard by swinging a kick directly at his knee. I opened my eyes in time to see it buckle, but he regained his balance quicker than I thought he would, and I had nowhere to go. Finally, I looked at him, and my blood froze.

"Doug?" My voice was merely a shriek full of breath and disbelief.

An unsettling chuckle rasped from him. "Just one of the names I use." He pinned his glare on me, amusement shining in his eyes. "Bet you didn't see that coming, did you?"

Without thinking, I kicked forward again, and he stumbled back a step before charging me with a curse. His hand whipped out, wrapping around my neck, and then he was sliding me up the cold metal wall behind me. My hair caught on little crevices, tearing from my scalp, but it was nothing compared to the pressure he put on my throat. It wasn't anything like Booker ever did to me; this was with the intent to kill me, not pleasure me.

My feet scrambled for purchase as he held me by my neck with both hands now, crushing my windpipe. My mind swirled with panic and the truth behind the fact that Doug wasn't who I thought he was—an innocent patron that frequented Marv's Diner.

"Hasn't anyone ever told you what happens when you don't listen?" His voice was so calm despite the pain he inflicted, so different from the man I knew before.

My mouth opened and closed as I tried to gasp for air, but nothing came.

"No?"

He waited as if I could answer.

Fucking prick.

"Then I have no choice but to show you what happens when you don't obey. Just like I showed that asshole I sent on a job what happens when he puts his hands on me in a display of theatrics."

I wasn't expecting it when he dropped me, and my body slammed to the hard floor. My shoulder screamed along with my lungs as I sucked in the oxygen I was starved of. But all too quickly, it was forced out of me when a boot hit me right in the stomach.

Not a single noise escaped me as I tried so hard to suck in air. I needed to breathe or I wouldn't fucking survive.

Breathe.

Breathe!

But my lungs were empty, and my stomach was heaving, and I was fucking dying.

I'm not dying.

I'm just scared.

That's it. It's the fear.

"Swallow your fear, Darlin'. Don't let it control you. Bend that fear to your advantage and use it as fuel."

Booker's voice filled my mind at the same time oxygen flowed into my lungs, his words fueling me to get it together. I wouldn't make it out of here if I let myself be weak.

The man crouched down in front of me, quietly watching as I gulped down air. His hands dangled in between his legs, his elbows propped on his thighs.

I continued to breathe heavily in the hopes it would make him think I was still struggling. And while I was—my lungs were still on fire, my throat burning, and my stomach sore—I needed him to think I was down if I wanted to get the upper hand here.

With a heaving chest, I quickly reeled my leg up and sent as much force as I could muster behind the kick, straight into his shin.

But before my foot could land true, he grabbed my ankle and squeezed.

"Such a feisty little thing," he said as I screamed. From pain or frustration, I wasn't sure.

His fingers dug into my skin as I tried to yank my leg back, but it was no use. I was at a disadvantage where I lay on my side.

He yanked me toward him, causing me to roll onto my back. I tried to twist onto my side again, but he was on me in a flash, and my entire body was instantly on alert as it hummed with panic.

His thighs straddled my hips, keeping my legs useless as I thrashed.

"Use your manners and maybe I'll take it easy."

I tried to rear my leg up again, but my knee only hit his backside with barely any force.

He was sitting up, watching as I struggled. The sick fuck fucking got off on it.

I needed my energy, and lying here wiggling around while it was clearly useless wouldn't get me anywhere. I stopped, staring up at him as I tried to catch my breath. "He's not coming for me, if that's what you're hoping."

The asshole smirked. "You underestimate how much power you hold over those boys."

I gritted my teeth together as I let out a strangled laugh. "You underestimate how much they actually care for me."

He tilted his head to the side. "Really?"

I waited, knowing he had more to say.

"I've seen them with you. But not just them—Booker."

"Booker would bury me himself if given the chance."

The thought alone had emotion threatening to swell my throat. I hated admitting how much I'd grown attached to him.

"Ah, see. He *doesn't* want to. Henley's a little fool, making it too easy to keep an eye on him. And, well, you know how the three of them live together. I have no choice but to have my men watching over Austin and Booker, too." He leaned closer, but I didn't try to shrink back, even if I could. It'd only fuel his satisfaction. "I know exactly how much that man cares for you, which made you the perfect hostage." He patted my cheek before sitting up again, looking bored. "But the thing about hostages is, it's only a fifty percent chance they'll make it out alive."

"Then kill me," I spit out. "What are you waiting for? If you're so certain he'll come for me, just kill me. He wouldn't know."

His eyes narrowed the slightest bit. "So eager to beg for your death."

"It's better than spending another minute in this van with you."

The corners of his mouth tilted up at that. "I thought you liked being manhandled?"

Bile threatened to creep up, but I shoved it down.

He chuckled, the sound low and vomit-inducing. "So easy to rile you up, Brynne."

"So what's your plan?" I asked, needing his weight off my body like a fish needed water. "Kill the both of us once he shows up?"

He shrugged. "I could. But it's a good thing you're a hostage, and you don't get that kind of information."

"You're just going to kill me anyway."

He leaned down again, bracing both hands on the floor right above my shoulders. "What's the fun without a little surprise?"

My lips were a thin line, my teeth threatening to break clean through.

His hand disappeared behind his back, and then cold metal pressed against my cheek, and I realized he'd pulled out a gun. My heart instantly pounded in my chest, and my mind spun as panic seized hold of me.

The man's eyes dropped to my lips as the bottom one quivered. "Sh, sh, sh. Don't be scared now." He trailed the gun down my cheek, across the curve of my jaw, then up to my mouth. He tugged my bottom lip down with the tip of the muzzle, and my entire body shook as my breaths came in heavy pants. "We wouldn't want your boyfriend to see his little girlfriend all worked up, would we?"

His eyes searched mine as he glided the cold metal down my chin and over my throat.

"Ah, who am I kidding?"

He pressed the gun to the side of my neck.

"I *want* him to see the life seep out of you."

Gravel crunched under tires outside, and the corner of his mouth ticked up.

"Just in time."

CHAPTER 22

BOOKER

Brynne's red bandana sat in a heap on my center console, and it was all I could think about as I sat around the corner from the park off the exit. I'd dropped Austin and Henley off to scope the area, and the plan was for me to pull into the parking lot alone. I didn't want to risk her life if Chase's boss got ticked off that I'd brought company.

Austin and Henley were the backup now, in case things went south on my end. Two men stood guard at the back of a black van. They each had their own gun tucked in the waistband of their jeans as they talked. If they'd looked hard enough, they would have seen my truck through the foliage, but to my advantage, they were distracted.

We were guessing Brynne was inside the van, so Austin's job was to take care of whoever the driver was, and Henley's was to deal with dipshit one and dipshit two at the back. I'd handle the boss and getting Brynne back. That was, if everything went to plan.

Every second I sat here was another second that something could be happening to her, and the thought made me sick. I couldn't wait any longer.

I reached across the center console and opened the glove box to pull out my pistol. Clicking the compartment shut again, I set the gun between my thighs and shifted into reverse. Slowly backing the truck up, I drove onto the main road and headed onto the street that led to the gravel parking lot. I turned into the abandoned park and killed my headlights as I rolled to a stop. I let it idle for a minute as the two men stared at me. They both donned their guns at the same time, keeping them low.

I killed the engine, taking one last glance at the bandana beside me as I hid the gun in my jeans below my shirt, then got out. I left the door open just in case they decided to fire, but I stepped out from the protection of it.

"Where is she." My tone left no room for question. I wanted my girl back, no matter what it took.

"Busy," the tall one said.

The van was still running, which didn't comfort me one fucking bit. I just had to trust that Austin would take care of whoever was behind the wheel before they had the chance to run.

I held my hands wide. "Well, I'm here."

As if on cue, the back door to the van opened, and a man clad in all black jumped out with a gun gripped in his hand. He barely spared me a glance before turning back around to grab something.

Panicked breaths sounded as he pulled, and that voice that made every nerve in my fucking body come alive filled my ears, wrapping around my mind, telling me to go to her. But I stood firm.

"Don't fucking touch me!" Brynne shouted as he yanked her to the edge of the van. Her feet hit the ground as he wrapped his free hand around her forearm, which was at an awkward angle as I noticed her arms were tied behind her back. As soon as she was on her feet, my eyes couldn't miss the blood coating the side of her face.

I stepped forward on instinct, but the short guy cocked his gun.

"What did you do to her?" I tried to keep my voice calm, but I couldn't be fucking serene seeing her hurt like that. I wanted to tear every fucking limb from their bodies, gut them like fucking pigs.

"Did what you couldn't do," the man with his filthy hand on my girl said. But I knew his fucking name. Same with all his different personas he put on for show. "Taught her to behave."

My sweatshirt was swimming on her, covering her shorts, and even from where I stood, I could see her legs shaking.

I rolled my lips together. "Doesn't seem like you did a very good job if she's still fighting you."

"We're working on that." He looked down at her, bringing the tip of the gun up to her cheek. She froze instantly, her wide eyes glued to me like I was her north star in this dark lot. "Aren't we, sweetheart?"

My blood boiled in my fucking veins. I'd never hated a sight so much in my life—her standing there like a deer in the headlights, like her death was imminent. I wouldn't let that be the outcome.

"What do you want?" I barked. I was done playing fucking games.

He dropped the gun back to his side, his finger on the trigger as he looked at me. "What I'm owed."

"You're not owed shit."

He tilted his head. "I'm not? Far as I know, Chase won a prize, and that prize was mine. Now it's gone. Pay up, and I might consider giving your little girlfriend back."

My jaw ached with how hard it was clenched. "Chase cheated."

The man's brows rose. "Is that so?"

"Everyone in that room can attest to it, so my deed isn't his, and it sure as hell isn't yours." *Neither is my Brynne.*

In my peripheral, Austin stepped out of the bushes, approaching the driver's side of the vehicle. I kept my eyes forward, not wanting to give away his position with their backs to him.

The boss shrugged. "He won it fair and square."

"That how you play, Lance?"

He tried to hide it, but I didn't miss the slight shock in his eyes at the use of his real name. He wasn't the only one who did his research.

"Fair and square?" I added, then tipped my chin up in Brynne's direction. "Doesn't look like you gave my girl much of a fair chance here, did you?"

Lance swallowed. I'd taken him off guard, just like I'd wanted. A smart man never left paperwork lying around with his name on it, but when we were digging through his house, I'd found an old letter from someone addressed to him, with his full name. It hadn't been hard to find every little thing out about him from there. How he ran away from home as a kid, or how his father was arrested for drunk driving. That his mother was a prostitute, and he had no records in terms of renting or jobs past the age of eighteen.

"Someone has to be the bad guy," Lance said as the tall guy took a step toward me. The old swing set behind them creaked as it swung in the wind while the dry leaves rustled above us.

I needed to keep stalling them. Keep him talking. I wouldn't be able to get Brynne away unharmed without Austin and Henley. Not with a trigger-happy man holding her.

Austin had disappeared inside the van without a sound, and I could only hope he'd taken care of his part of the plan.

I rubbed at a callus on my hand, inspecting it like it hadn't been there for the last thirty or so years. "See, that's the problem, Lance. You're playing a part in being a bad guy." I looked up again, meeting his gaze. "But I'm not acting." I moved a hand to my shirt as if I was simply rubbing an itch. "I *am* the fucking villain." In one swift motion, the pistol was in my hand, and I was taking aim at Lance.

One after the other, Henley put a bullet in the two guys' skulls after emerging from the brush. They both fell to the ground with a thud, and then Austin was swinging open the doors to the van. One hit Lance in the back, causing him to lose balance, but he held tight to Brynne in return, keeping himself upright. My bullet flew past him, right at the fucking taillight as I shifted my aim at the last second. It wasn't worth accidentally hitting Brynne.

Brynne's scream rang through the air, and panic seized me with the thought that I may have hit her instead, but then the glass shattered to pieces with a pop, and the tiniest bit of relief hit me. But it came all too soon as Lance backed up with Brynne's back now pressed to his chest. He had the muzzle of his gun pressed to the side of her head, staining the tip with her blood.

"I'll kill her right fucking here if you don't back the fuck off!" Lance yelled, backing up another few steps.

Austin hopped down from the van with his gun still gripped in his hands. He glanced at me, as if I knew what to fucking do. Whatever we did, it had to end in Brynne getting out of here alive. If anyone was getting a fucking bullet in their head tonight, it was Lance.

"Let her go, Lance," I warned, keeping my gun trained on him. I couldn't shoot, though. Not with Brynne being used as a shield.

Tears streamed down her face, and one glance at her exposed neck sent blackness careening into my line of vision. Her fragile skin was bruised a gruesome shade of purple, and she'd barely been with them for half an hour.

"I want what's mine!" he barked.

"Then we'll trade," I said.

He shook his head. "I have no fucking reason to trust you."

"And neither do I. But she means a hell of a lot more to me than some fucking piece of property." Just saying the words out loud felt odd. Never in a million years would I have thought I'd think so highly of a woman to give up everything for her, but for Brynne, I would. I'd grown attached too damn fast, but I didn't regret a thing.

"How do I know you have it with you?" Lance asked.

"Austin will get it from my truck." He was the one

closest to the two of them, but it'd drop Lance's guard down enough for me to take him by surprise.

"Booker," Austin protested at the same time Henley sent me a questioning glance.

"Now, Austin. It's in my glove box." But all that was there was another magazine filled with bullets.

He glanced between Lance and me twice before giving in and dropping his gun. He walked toward the passenger side of my truck, careful not to make any sudden movements. Lance kept his eyes on Austin the entire way, making sure he didn't get any smart ideas, but he was looking at the wrong guy. Just like I'd expected he would.

I had one opportunity, and if I wasn't extremely precise with my aim, Brynne would suffer the consequences.

That wasn't something I was willing to let happen, so when I raised my pistol in their direction, with Lance's attention still focused on Austin at my truck, I centered all my hopes and wishes on the trajectory of the bullet.

My finger squeezed the trigger, and then my heart stopped.

CHAPTER 23

BRYNNE

The shot rang through the night air, and not even a second later, the deadly grip on my arm disappeared. I stood frozen, my gaze focused on the gravel faintly illuminated by the full moon. My ears rang, my mind spun, and every part of me screamed to run.

Boots crunched over gravel at a sprint, and then strong arms wrapped around me, pulling me away from the body that I knew surely lay behind me.

"Brynne," Booker's voice echoed, piercing my foggy mind.

He dropped his arms, placing his rough-yet-comforting hands on my cheeks. I couldn't see, but my eyes were open.

Lance was going to kill me.

"Brynne," Booker repeated, and then someone was behind me, grabbing my hand.

I shrieked, my heart instantly threatening to beat itself into oblivion as I wanted to dart away. To be free from the fear that enveloped every one of my senses in this moment.

"Brynne, it's okay." Booker's hands were on my shoulders, giving me no choice but to look at him as my vision finally let him in. "Austin is just going to cut the rope, okay? He's not going to hurt you. I won't let anyone hurt you."

I nodded, swallowing the panic that still strangled my sore throat.

Booker's hands slid up my neck to my cheeks again as his eyes roamed over me. I fought my instinct to run, instead standing as still as my trembling body would let me while Austin went back to working at the rope that burned my wrists. Once he cut through it, my hands fell to my sides. My shoulders ached as I looked down at the raw skin just below my hands.

With a delicate finger, Booker hooked my hair behind my ear to better survey my face. "Brynne, baby, what did they do to you?" His voice was merely a whisper, and it didn't beg for an answer. One look at me and he could see the damage inflicted. They all could.

I sucked in a breath when he prodded the wound on my head, and a crease formed between his brows. Our eyes met, and I saw all the pain glistening bright as day in his. He'd been...worried. And I felt like shit for thinking he wouldn't come. I'd been desperate, scared, and I didn't want to put my bets on something that might not happen. But he'd come for me. *Killed* for me. And not for the first time.

I didn't hear as Henley approached, but saw the outstretched bottle of water. I raised a shaking hand to take it from him. "Thank you." The two words were hoarse, and almost hurt to get out.

He dipped his chin in a nod, and I got the feeling he thought this was all his fault. But I didn't blame him for any of this. My being here, abducted and injured, was no one's doing but Lance's, and thankfully, he was now bleeding out mere feet behind us.

I didn't uncap the water. Instead, my focus stayed on my wrists where the skin was broken, bruised, and bloody. Had I really struggled that hard? Given Lance the satisfaction that I was at his mercy?

Booker forced my attention back to him. "Hey. Look at me."

I did, and then all I wanted to do was melt into him.

"Are you hurt anywhere else?" Booker asked.

The question itself was loaded, as I wasn't sure where on my body I didn't ache or burn.

With my hand not holding the bottle, I slowly brought it to my side where Lance had kicked me, but I didn't look down as Booker did. His jaw pulsed before he grabbed my hand, wrapping his warm palm around mine. Then, with his other, he lifted the hem of the sweatshirt.

I knew it was bad when he hissed in a breath.

"Does it hurt to breathe?" he asked.

To make sure, I inhaled deeply, but only a little pinch of pain followed. I shook my head. My gaze found Austin's where he stood off to the side. Sympathy was written all over him. They felt guilty, like this was somehow their fault.

"I'm taking you to the hospital," Booker said, letting the sweatshirt fall to cover my stomach again.

My body instantly began to shake with the thought of him not being by my side. What would I tell the nurses if they asked how I got these injuries? They'd assume Booker did it, and I couldn't bear them pinning this on him.

"N-no," I stammered. My bare legs were feeling the chill

from the fall air now that the adrenaline was beginning to wear off.

"Brynne, you're hurt. I'm taking you," Booker said adamantly.

"They're going to t-take me from you."

He shook his head, pulling me to his chest. I leaned all my weight on him as I breathed him in. "I won't let them do that. I'll be by your side the entire time."

My fingers tangled in the fabric of his shirt. "Do you p-promise?"

I felt his chin brush the top of my head, his stubble getting caught in my hair as he nodded. "I promise."

———

"Only six stitches. Not as bad as I thought," Dr. Manson said, setting the tools he'd used to sew up the side of my head on the metal tray beside him. "Keep the wound dry for about forty-eight hours, and then you can gently clean the area."

"And the bruising on her neck?" Booker asked. He'd stayed by my side the whole time, just like he'd promised. His hand never left mine.

Dr. Manson turned to him on his swivel stool. "She should try to keep talking to a minimum, and sleep with her head elevated to reduce any swelling. Ice will help, too."

Booker nodded in response. He'd done most of the talking since we arrived, but it'd been difficult trying to make the nurse understand I didn't want to be away from him when she wanted to question what happened. We'd gone with a story that I was mugged and the guy got away. Though the nurse didn't look convinced, she hadn't prodded. For obvious reasons, we wouldn't be filing a report.

Austin and Henley had stayed behind to take care of the mess. Booker had received a few updates from them after they left the abandoned park with the bodies in the van, but other than that, he'd left them to deal with all of it. I should've encouraged him to go help, but I was selfish and wanted him here with me. Booker wasn't complaining about it, either.

Dr. Manson set a reassuring hand on the bar next to my arm. "Rest, pain meds, and water. Keep on that routine for a few weeks, and you'll be good as new in no time."

He'd advised to stay in bed as much as possible to heal my cracked rib from when Lance kicked me, and I wanted nothing more than to do just that. So long as Booker was by my side.

"Thank you," I said, my voice still gravelly.

Dr. Manson nodded in our direction, then left the room, closing the door behind him.

Booker's thumb brushed over the back of my hand. "I really hate to ask this, Darlin'..."

I cocked my head in question.

His eyes looked pained. "Do you want the nurse to do a rape kit?"

I swallowed wrong the second he said it and erupted in a fit of coughs. He thought they'd...

"No," I answered after I got the cough under control. "Plus, I was only mugged, remember?"

I tried to smile at that, but Booker didn't find it amusing at all.

"I wanted his death to be slower," he admitted, quieting his voice so only I could hear him.

"I know." I wanted the same.

"But you were the only thing that mattered in that moment, Brynne. Not revenge, not my rage. You."

I pressed my lips together to keep the tears at bay. "I know."

He shook his head as he moved his gaze to our hands locked together. "You don't know."

"Then tell me," I whispered. I wanted all of him. His thoughts, secrets, confessions. Every bit of him, I craved.

"I don't want to share you anymore." His eyes met mine again, likely to gauge my reaction. "Fuck, I don't know why I did in the first place. We were just toying with each other, and I fucking liked the way you looked all exposed to them... But now, it makes me want to throw up."

I leaned forward slightly, ignoring the pinch of pain in my torso. I set a palm against his cheek. "I don't want you to share me anymore, either."

His brows pulled together. "You don't?"

I shook my head. "It was fun, but I only have eyes for you, Booker. No one else."

Something shifted inside him, and then he was on his feet and leaning into my space, crashing his lips to mine as he let go of my hand.

We didn't kiss much, but when we did, it was explosive. Our tongues were like live rounds of TNT, and the second they sparked together, we ignited.

He was careful as our lips meshed together, keeping his

hands off me. But even now, I wanted nothing more than for him to touch me.

Booker pulled back, immediately sliding his hand back into mine. "Let's go home."

The corners of my mouth tilted up at the idea of it being our home.

Sharing the place we lived with Austin and Henley didn't bother me. My eyes were only on Booker.

They always were.

CHAPTER 24

BRYNNE

My phone rang for the twelfth time as Booker helped me up the porch steps.

"You might as well just answer it," he said, opening the front door.

I walked past him, his hand still glued to my lower back like if he removed it, I'd break into a million pieces and have no hope of being whole again.

"I don't know what to say to her." *Hey, McKenna. Sorry for disappearing tonight. I was knocked out, shoved in the back of a van, and held hostage by some maniac who wanted the deed to Booker's ranch. Oh, and if anybody asks, tell them I was simply mugged.*

The door clicked shut behind us, and then he was helping ease me up the stairs. I could think about food later. I just wanted to curl up under the covers and sleep for fifteen years.

"The truth." He said it like it was that simple.

"She'd freak."

"Or she'd do what any best friend would and be there for you."

He was right. She'd never treated me like I couldn't tell her anything and everything. She hadn't even blinked when I told her about my agreement with Booker. Any other person would've judged me, but McKenna stood by and supported my every decision. What had happened to me tonight was out of my hands, and she'd understand.

"I'll call her while you make me food," I decided, knowing he'd force a meal on me even if I refused.

We hit the second floor, and he led me down the hall to his bedroom. I assumed I'd no longer have my own room here, given at this point, we were officially together. There'd be no point in spending a night without him from this day forward.

At my side, Booker raised a brow. "Is that so?"

"Mhmm. I think I'm feeling pasta."

He chuckled, the sound low as it wrapped around my heartstrings. "If that's what my darlin' requests." He reached out a hand, swinging his door open. "Bath before you call her?"

Though all I wanted was to lie down, I wasn't in the best hygienic state. I nodded, and he left me on the cushioned bench in the bedroom while he filled the tub with steaming water.

Once the bath was ready, he helped me undress, then got in the water behind me. I leaned back against his chest, enjoying the warmth as it seeped into my aching, bruised skin.

The wet tips of his fingers glided up and down my forearm as I closed my eyes.

"You're beautiful, Brynne," he murmured.

My eyelids opened as I tilted my head back slightly to get a good look at him. "Did you just compliment me without your dick inside me?"

He frowned, which caused a smile to bloom on my lips. "Careful, Darlin'. Don't encourage me."

Just the thought alone had my core heating. "Well, I'm not *that* hurt."

He shook his head, shooting the idea down. "I'm not risking it. In a week, we'll talk."

My mouth popped open. "A week?"

"You should be glad I'm not saying until the end of your healing."

I shrugged, relaxing my back against his warm chest again. "Wouldn't matter if you did. I couldn't possibly stay away that long."

"Some might say that's a little obsessive so soon into our relationship."

My cheeks heated slightly at the use of the label. "They'd say the same about you breaking into my motel room wearing a mask."

His heart fluttered at my back. "You liked it, though."

That smile stayed stuck to my face as I admitted, "I did."

———

The door squeaked open, and McKenna's face appeared in the crack. As soon as she saw I was awake, she opened it wider and slipped inside. She shut it behind her, then crossed to the bed. "Brynne, I'm so sorry—"

"Don't apologize," I cut her off. "This wasn't your fault."

"I should have stayed with you instead of getting caught up with Grace."

She sat on the bed beside me, taking in the bruises littering my neck. Then, her eyes trailed to the stitches, and she winced. "I'm so sorry."

"McKenna." I reached out, grabbing her hand. I was in one of Booker's t-shirts with shorts on underneath, and only had the sheet over my legs. My back was propped up against the pillows so I could eat easier once Booker brought my dinner up. "None of this was your fault."

The door opened again, and this time, Austin and Henley entered. They'd wanted to check on me after my bath, but Booker had told them to wait so I could have a few minutes alone before McKenna got here.

McKenna's eyes immediately narrowed on Henley, and she shot off the bed, aiming right for him. I instantly regretted telling her the little information I did. "You." She raised a hand, her feet stomping the ground, but before her slap could land true on Henley, Austin grabbed her wrist.

Austin walked her back a step. "Calm down, vicious kitten. No need to get the claws out."

"He's the reason that son of a bitch even had his sights on her in the first place!" she yelled.

I flinched, because she was right. But I didn't blame him. What happened happened, and pinning the blame on someone when there was nothing they could do to change the past was a waste of energy.

McKenna tried to wrench her wrist free, but once she

figured out it was no use, she threw her whole body at Austin. He had no choice but to wrap his arms around her.

"Just one fucking slap!" she complained. "That's all I want!"

"Not happening," Austin said.

She groaned in frustration, then acted like she was done. Austin waited a moment before loosening his hold on her, and in a flash, she was trying to dart for Henley again. Henley stepped to the side, watching as Austin hefted McKenna up over his shoulder.

Her fists came down on his back. "Put me down, you fucking caveman!"

He carried her to the opposite side of the room from Henley, who still stood by the door. "Stop trying to attack my friend and I might."

He plopped her down in the chair, bracing both hands on the armrests on either side of her to keep her planted.

"You know you want to hurt him for it, too," she said, trying to quiet how loud her voice had gotten in her rage.

"I want to do a lot of things to a lot of people, kitten, but it ain't going to get me anywhere by doing it."

She glared up at him, her blonde hair loose and tangled around her shoulders from the mayhem. "You're a dick."

He shoved off the chair to stand in front of her. "Call me what you want. I know how you really feel."

Instantly, her cheeks turned to twin flames, and she was darting out of the chair. This time, at him. He caught her around the waist, lifting her a foot off the ground before throwing her back into the chair.

"Stop doing that!" she screamed in frustration.

"You first," he spit back.

I couldn't help but laugh, which made all the focus in the room turn to me. I pressed a palm to my side as my giggling ebbed, and Booker slipped in the door with a tray.

"What the fuck is going on in here? Sounds like a goddamn jungle from downstairs," Booker said, and then he saw the placement of my hand and rushed toward me. "What's wrong? Does it hurt?"

I smiled again, biting back my laugh as I shook my head. "Couldn't feel better."

McKenna never failed to make a shitty situation better, and this was proof of it.

My eyes moved to what was in the bowl, and my smile grew. "Alfredo is my favorite."

"I know. It's all you ever order at the diner," Booker said.

"How do you know that?"

He shot a wink my way. "I know everything, Darlin'. Including that you need to eat this and get some rest. Which means everyone needs to get the fuck out." He turned his glare on Austin and Henley.

"I'm staying," McKenna said, no room for argument in her tone.

"We have a guest room down the hall if you want to spend the night," Booker said, because I knew damn well he wanted to be the one by my side tonight.

She nodded, standing from the chair. "It's a good thing I always keep a to-go bag in my car."

"Need help bringing it up?" Austin asked like the gentleman he was.

She sent a death-glare his way. "I can handle my own bag. Thanks."

Henley gave McKenna a wide berth as she left the room. Austin had his hands up in mock surrender. "Don't know what I did to piss that one off."

Booker set the tray on my lap as I said, "She's nice to customers, some family, and me. That's about it."

Austin groaned, rolling his neck. "Any way I can ask that she not come over often? Or at all works, too."

I picked up the fork, wanting nothing more than to devour this bowl of pasta and cuddle up next to Booker for the rest of the night. "Not gonna happen. Sorry."

Austin's lips pressed together in a tight line. "Great."

Henley and Austin left the room, closing the door behind them to give us some privacy. Booker slid under the covers beside me and fiddled around with the remote, trying to find a show to watch while I ate.

I eyed the way he studied the remote. "Have you never worked a TV before?"

He glanced my way. "Don't got much time for TV, Darlin'."

"Let me guess. Ranch chores."

He pressed the menu button on the remote, squinting his eyes at the big screen to make sure it pulled up what he wanted it to. "You're lucky you're injured or I'd make you regret that little comment."

"I'll start a list so you can dole out the punishment later."

Booker smirked, then settled on a cooking show. He shared bites of my giant bowl of pasta, and once I was done, he made sure I drank an entire glass of water and took my pain medication. Finally, our bodies wrapped around each other under the comforter, and we fell asleep to the sound of coyotes howling somewhere out on the property.

In Booker's arms, I was safe, but in the way that kept my heart racing and my mind on the edge of its seat. He was fear itself and a warm blanket wrapped in one.

And though what we had was new and uncertain, I had no doubt that he'd never let another person put their hands on me again. We were an unlikely pairing, but we were right for each other.

And that was all that mattered.

EPILOGUE

BRYNNE

T*wo weeks later...*

"Do I get to have my own horse one day?" I asked, glancing over at Booker where he rode beside me on his horse, Onyx.

"That what you want, Darlin'?" His voice was gruff from being up way too late with me, but regardless, he still got out of our bed at four a.m. sharp to start work on the ranch.

I looked down at the gray under me, admiring her long mane and speckled coat. I let out a thoughtful hum. "Maybe."

Booker adjusted his gloved hand on the rein as the sun set in the distance, casting a warm orange glow over the yellowing grass surrounding us for miles. "Whatever you want, just say the words, and I'll make it happen."

I cocked a brow in his direction, peeling my eyes away from the mare as she stepped over cow pies. "This side of you is weird."

He let out a hoarse chuckle, turning that dark gaze on me. Instantly, I was starving for the taste of him. "What side?"

I waved a hand at him. "This...caring side."

Under his full beard, he smiled. "Don't like when I spoil you, huh?"

I shook my head.

"What do you like, then?"

I fought the urge to curl the sides of my lips up, but there was no way to stop the heat that crept up my neck. "That's a loaded question."

He studied me, then reached a hand over to gently tug my reins back to stop the horse. Onyx followed suit, and Booker had him sidestep so his stirrup was touching my leg. He released the rein, moving to grab the back of my neck. The bruises had faded completely in the last couple weeks, and Booker had somewhat kept his promise of staying away for one week. He'd taken to giving me orgasms in his bed only, and after seven days, he finally gave me what I craved behind the barn. He'd sunk his cock so deep inside me, my body had taken forever to adjust to the size of him again. He'd been so gentle, too. Like he was scared I might shatter to pieces in his arms if he tore his eyes away from mine for merely a second.

That night stuck with him the same it did with me, but I was convinced he was more affected by my disappearance than I was. I'd gone through my share of waking from nightmares, but so did he. When my gaze found him in the parking lot that night, I'd never seen the man look so...petrified. Like his world was chipping away piece by piece, threatening to crumble completely if I stopped breathing life into it.

Since then, we'd declared that would never be a possibility. We'd be together through this life—no matter how quickly things progressed.

Sometimes, you just knew. And with Booker, it felt right.

"I've got all the time in the world to listen, Darlin'," he said.

I nearly laughed. "I want my broody rancher back. You're starting to freak me out."

The ghost of a smirk crested his lips, and then he was sliding a hand into the saddle bag on the opposite side of the saddle right as a cloud floated in front of the dimming sun.

"Your wish is my command."

My eyes fell to the mask in his hand as he lifted it. Removing his cowboy hat, he adjusted the mask over his face, then set the hat back on his head.

"Much better," I teased as a crack of thunder rolled in the distance.

He reached out, threading his fingers through my hair. "Which do you prefer more?" He gave a small tug, sending goosebumps up my arms as his fingertips ghosted my scalp. "Gentle?" Then, his grip changed, and he was pulling my head back by my hair, exposing my neck. "Or rough?"

A gasp escaped me as he brought his face closer to my neck, inhaling deeply. "Both," I replied.

"And which do you want right now?"

My core heated, and I wanted nothing more than to

clench my thighs to alleviate some of the ache, but that would only make the horse move, and I needed to stay put. To keep Booker's hands on me.

"Rough," I managed to get out on a breath.

"That's my girl." His fingers tightened the slightest before he released me, and then he was dismounting. He slid the bit out of Onyx's mouth, then clicked his tongue and patted the horse's ass. He took off at a gallop, heading back in the direction of the barn.

I swiveled in the saddle to watch Onyx disappear. "How are you going to get back?" My sentence ended on a yelp as Booker lifted me off the horse.

"We'll ride together," he said simply as I wrapped my legs around his waist.

He still had the bridle looped over his shoulder as he lowered me to the ground. He gently laid my head in the plush grass, his weight a welcome pressure. As if he couldn't help himself, he shoved the mask up his face to reveal his mouth and began peppering slow kisses down the side of my neck to my collarbone. "Anything you want," he repeated in between kisses. "Say the words, and I'll do it."

He'd been like this since the night I was taken and nearly killed. Treating me like the most delicate shell on a beach full of abrasive sand. Like one wrong move, and I might shatter. With him, I didn't think that was possible. He held my head above water when all I wanted to do was sink some days, and every day, I'd gotten better—mentally and physically. But those demons still lurked in his mind. I tried not to feel guilty for it, but it was no secret he felt this way because of what happened to me.

"A dog," I said, to which his lips froze on my skin before he lifted himself slightly to peer down at me.

"A dog?"

I nodded, a smile pulling at my lips. "I want a dog."

His cowboy hat fell to the grass as he pulled his mask off the rest of the way to get a better look at me. Once he decided I was being serious, he said, "We'll have to talk to the guys."

A gasp escaped me as my smile widened. "We can really get a dog?"

"If that's what you want—"

Before he could finish his sentence, I was shoving all my body weight at him to get him onto his back. I rolled on top of him, sprinkling kisses all over his cheeks, nose, and forehead. "Thank you, thank you, thank you."

Booker let out a chuckle. "Have you never had a dog before?"

I shook my head, ceasing my kisses. "My mother always said they were too messy and I didn't want it to be outside all the time."

"Messes can be cleaned," he declared, hooking a lock of hair behind my ear.

"You've proved that a time or two," I muttered.

He threaded his fingers into my hair in response to my dig, then tugged my head toward his. Before our lips could meet, I was shoving at his chest. "We need to go talk to Austin and Henley."

He propped up on his elbows as I stood, staring at me. "Can't wait until tomorrow?"

I popped a hip, waiting for him to get up.

With another low chuckle, he moved to stand, grabbing his mask and cowboy hat off the ground. As I turned for my horse, he caught me by the waist, spinning me around so that my chest was pressed to his. "The lady gets what the lady wants."

"Because I'm *your* lady."

"Damn right, Darlin'. No one else's."

After a kiss I lost myself in, we mounted the horse together and rode back to the barn to find Onyx waiting for us by the gate. Once Booker untacked them and sent them back into the pasture, we headed inside the house to find Austin and Henley playing a game of cards at the kitchen island.

"What's that grin for?" Austin asked, peering up at me from his hand.

I couldn't help myself as I bounced on the balls of my feet. "We're getting a dog."

Henley glanced over his shoulder at us, setting down his cards. "A dog?"

I nodded. "Mhmm. Booker said we could get one, but we wanted to make sure it was okay with you guys."

Austin glanced at Henley, a silent discussion passing between the two of them with the act.

"What?" I asked as a crease formed between Booker's brows.

"We actually wanted to talk to you guys about something, too," Austin started with another glance in Henley's direction.

"Well, fucking spit it out, then," Booker demanded.

Austin gnawed on his bottom lip before saying, "We

were thinking of putting two double-wides on the property so you two could have your space in the house."

"Yeah. Plus, I hate dogs," Henley added.

My jaw dropped in Henley's direction, as if that was the more surprising information of the two.

"Is that really what you want to do?" Booker asked.

I looked up at him, finding the set of his jaw hard and his eyes slightly worried. Like he didn't want to be the reason they moved out of the house.

I set a hand on his arm, giving him a reassuring squeeze. "They'll still be on the property."

"Yeah," Austin confirmed. "We won't be far at all, and we have the extra land to spare for it."

Booker's throat worked on a swallow. I never thought I'd see the man get emotional over his two best friends, but here we were.

"You guys can take all the time you need with the process," I said, filling in for the words Booker wasn't voicing.

Henley dipped his chin. "Takes a couple months to get them delivered out here, anyway."

"You'll have us here to annoy you guys for a good bit still," Austin said, as if that was what Booker would be missing by them moving out.

Booker gave a hesitant nod, words still failing on his tongue.

"So..." Henley began. "What kind of dog?"

"I thought you hated dogs," I reminded him.

Henley pressed his lips into a thin line. "Doesn't mean I'm not nosey."

Finally, Booker shifted his stance and said, "How soon can you move out?"

Then we joined them in their game as the night passed us by, nothing but a distant howl and sprinkling rain to be heard over our laughter and teasing.

THE END

Acknowledgments

Okay. Wow. I genuinely have no idea where to start with these acknowledgements. Usually, I just *know*. But this being my first dark romance, I feel I have a lot of important people to thank for believing in me with this idea.

First of all—Rose. You're basically the entire reason I decided to take the leap into the dark side. I wanted to for so long, but in true Karley fashion, I didn't feel qualified enough. As if one can be "qualified" to write a specific plot, or genre, or anything. Heck, we make all this up in our minds! You planted the seed, I ran with it, and the book was plotted in literally hours. Maybe less than an hour. I can't remember, but what I do remember is the absolute wild ride this book has put me on, and I can't get off. I won't get off. It's an addiction, and the dark side has claimed me. So thank you, beautiful Rose, for being my PA through this crazy journey and supporting me every step of the way. This one is for you, in every way shape and form.

Bobbi, Bobniss, my wonderful editor and best friend. You sat by my side at our writer's retreat and helped me work out the nitty gritty with this book baby. You listened to my voice memos, like you always do, with my wild ideas. My "should I do this or that"'s. You make being an indie author a little less lonely, and I love and appreciate the friendship that has blossomed between us in the past

YEAR. A year, I have known you, and for infinite more, I will keep you. Sorry, I don't make the rules.

My bestie for the restie, Kate. You surely didn't help with this dark side transition—no, you only egged it on, and boy am I glad that you did. I remember standing on my back porch sending you a voice memo saying "I think I'm just going to write it. What's the worst that could happen?" And you said "do it" and I did and now look?! Crazy how that happens. Thank you for fueling the dark side of my mind and always being my morning podcast. We're getting that damn porch and wine, I'm shouting it into the universe.

Lainey Lawson. I told you my crazy idea to do a little dark novella, and you supported me from the get go. Some might think cowboy romance brought us together, but it was really suspense. Don't lie. We're sluts for suspense, it's just the way it is. So I hope you enjoyed the action, the smut, and the quick read.

My family, I love you. Probably don't read this, but I love you.

My baddies, Dany, Mollie, Sarah, Addey, Maria, Kat, and of course, Bobbi. Thank you for inviting me on my first ever writer's retreat. I truly found such a beautiful friendship in all of you, and I'm so dang glad you're all in my life. Without the retreat, I probably wouldn't have had the balls to start my fantasy or this dark novella, so thank you for not only inspiring me to step out of my comfort zone, but reminding me that good things can happen when you do.

My beta readers, Katie one, Katie two, Tiffany, Rose, Maeghen, Hunter, and Dani, I appreciate the heck out of you guys. As always, you help make my stories stronger, and

I wish I could give you all the world for the efforts you put into my books. Thank you for taking time out of your days to read my words and support me.

My ARC readers, thank you for reading my books and shouting about them from the rooftops. I truly cannot sum up in words how much I appreciate every single one of you. You make this dream of mine possible, and I'm eternally grateful for it.

Thank you to my street team for supporting me. Whether it through posts, shares, a like, or a conversation, you're my dream team, and I'm so glad I have all of you to share amazing news with and scream over teasers with. It truly makes my day when you guys are as excited for my books and reveals as I am. Thank you for making me feel a little less small in an ocean of amazing talent.

Thank you to Kim at the Author Buddy for making the most absolutely perfect cover for this novella. I couldn't have imagined anything better than this for Booker and Brynne.

I'm probably forgetting people because my memory is the worst, but just know that if we talk, or heck, you just read my books or share a post or two, I'm so dang thankful for you. Thank you to everyone reading this for making my dreams come true.

xo Karley

More books by Karley Brenna

Standalone
Wasted Memories

Bell Buckle series
Spur of the Moment
Beat around the Bush
Scrape the Barrel

About the Author

Karley Brenna lives in a small town in the middle of nowhere out west with her fiancé, son, and herd of pets. Her hobbies include writing, reading countless books heavy on romance, and listening to country music for hours. If she's not at home, she's either at a bookstore or getting lost in the hills on horseback. To stay up to date with Karley's future projects, follow her on social media @authorkarleybrenna.

Made in United States
Orlando, FL
03 November 2024

53448484R00161